Death by Publication

Death by Publication

A MYSTERY

J. J. Fiechter

ARCADE PUBLISHING • NEW YORK

Arcade Publishing books may be purchased in bulk at special discounts for sales promotion, corporate gifts, fund-raising, or educational purposes. Special editions can also be created to specifications. For details, contact the Special Sales Department, Arcade Publishing, 307 West 36th Street, 11th Floor, New York, NY 10018 or arcade@skyhorsepublishing.com.

Arcade Publishing® is a registered trademark of Skyhorse Publishing, Inc.®, a Delaware corporation.

Visit our website at www.arcadepub.com.

10 9 8 7 6 5 4 3 2 1

Library of Congress Cataloging-in-Publication Data is available on file.

ISBN: 978-1-61145-794-0

Printed in the United States of America

To Zic and Nours

"Noblesse Oblige"

But our hatred is almost indistinguishable from our love.
—Virginia Woolf, *The Waves*

Death by Publication

Chapter 1

Should one believe in premonitions? This morning, while I was still half asleep, I thought I heard a switch click on that would start the wheels of destruction turning.

I didn't even try to banish the evil spirits from my mind. With my eyes closed, I let them do their demonic dance in my mind, chanting over and over again: "Nicolas Fabry is going to win the Goncourt Prize. . . . Nicolas Fabry is going to win the Goncourt Prize. . . ." And in my heart of hearts I knew the evil spirits were right.

The pale morning light cast a mournful pall over the already distressing furniture of my hotel room. I had made it a habit over the past several years to take an autumn trip to France, to Vichy more specifically, to escape the all-pervasive London fog, but this time I had managed to bring the fog along with me. It was All Saints' Day, and beyond the hotel-room curtains a blanket of fog all but obscured the garden paths. The fog was a dirty gray, the color of my bitterness at knowing that Nicolas was going to walk away with that most prestigious of literary prizes, the Goncourt. Last night every radio station I tuned in to was proclaiming that Nicolas was the odds-on favorite. Which should have delighted me, for not only had I anticipated it, I had counted on it. It was my fate hanging in the balance, too, and Nicolas's victory was essential to my plan. Now all I had to do was find the courage to carry it out. But I was depressed, and everything I did only made it worse: walks in the well-manicured Vichy parks, which were still green despite the season; the firemen's concerts in the colonnaded park bandstands; even the sacrosanct spa waters. Nothing worked.

The telephone wake-up call roused me from my half sleep.

"Good morning, Sir Edward. It's seven-thirty."

I ordered a hearty breakfast — orange juice, tea, eggs and bacon, buttered toast. I was famished. Then I drew a bath. Today I had to have all my wits about me. Especially today. My visit to Vichy had not been a resounding success. I looked at myself in the bathroom mirror, and the image that stared back at me was hardly flattering: my skin had a leaden cast to it, and there were deep dark circles under my eyes. And yet I detected a bright new spark. Or, rather, a spark that had long been missing and was back again. Despite the solemnity — indeed, the dead seriousness — of the moment, I could not refrain from smiling at the mirrored image. I was smiling at the thought that soon, very soon, there would be a complete reversal of roles,

2

of which I would be the architect. Or should I say author? All things considered, even though I looked a little green around the gills, I wasn't all that bad looking, I decided. True, the hairline was receding, but it made me look serious, even distinguished. And those green eyes were not something you ran into every day. Stop being so hard on yourself, Edward. If only you took the trouble, you could be as attractive and seductive as anyone. You too had a writing talent. So you've just turned fifty and haven't yet written your masterpiece. Who says you still can't? And speaking of masterpieces, just because Nicolas Fabry's previous novels have been best-sellers doesn't make them masterpieces. In fact, it probably proves they weren't.

The room-service waiter knocked on the door and brought in my breakfast tray. Portuguese, I knew from his previous visits. Thin as a reed, and all buttoned up in his pin-striped hotel uniform. I looked at him as if at someone in a window display. I didn't even greet the man, and as he was leaving the room I snapped my fingers at him imperiously, a throwback to my years in Egypt. He turned around, annoyed.

"Sorry," I said, holding out a fifty-franc note as tip.

He pocketed the bill, then said very formally, in heavily accented English, "Thank you, Sir Edward." His use of my title and my own language pardoned my lack of tact, but I had been warned: from now on I would have to be constantly on the alert. The least little slip or loss of self-control could be my undoing. To date I had an almost legendary reputation for being even tempered, displaying at all times the stolid

3

impassivity of the English aristocracy. Now was certainly not the time to deviate from it.

By eight-thirty I had paid my bill. A taxi was waiting for me outside the hotel, and I clambered into it with an uncharacteristic feeling of urgency. Was it possible I was running a fever? I was boiling hot, and the taxi seat was full of uncomfortable ridges. The driver seemed to be driving with deliberate slowness. I was sure I was going to miss my train, and I began to drum my fingers on the back of the front seat, which doubtless irritated the man. He too was Arab, just like Yasmina. Yasmina . . .

In fact I almost did miss my train. I barely had time to grab an armful of newspapers and magazines at the station and hop onto the train before the doors closed behind me. I stowed my valise on the luggage rack of the compartment, then settled down and began to peruse the weekly news magazines, more to take my mind off my anxiety than to find out what was going on in the world. It wasn't all that easy. The first magazine I opened, *Paris Match*, had as its cover story a long article on — who else? — Nicolas Fabry.

The photographs themselves should have sufficed to double the magazine's circulation. What woman could have resisted that limpid, knowing gaze, which burrowed straight into the viewer's soul; or that winning smile, with just the right mixture of swagger and self-deprecation; or that brow, crowned by dark curly hair, that bespoke the conquering hero? The carefully clipped beard was to my mind a trifle ridiculous, but it rounded out the image. Operation Narcissus. Carefully crafted casual, in my view. The photos had been taken several months earlier, at Fabry's villa on the Riviera. The choicest part of the Riviera, I should add. You could see the Mediterranean pines in the near background, and in the distance the sparkling blue sea itself. The subject himself was sportily dressed, but he was wearing a tie, which was pulled down and slightly askew below the open collar of the shirt. Early in the interminable interview, Fabry revealed himself to be scandalously nonchalant about his "career." Could he comment for the readers about his years as a diplomat? There wasn't much to say, really. He had been in the diplomatic corps, true, but that was a long time ago, and besides, it was in another country. Sir Edward wondered how many readers, if any, would get Fabry's not-so-subtle allusion to T. S. Eliot. Next the man would be comparing himself to Joyce. Or maybe Proust. The diplomatic phase of his life, Fabry confided to the interviewer, had been due more to chance than to family tradition. But from his earliest diplomatic assignments on, his official functions had interfered with the creativity he had always felt welling up within him.

What followed was less interview than personal confession, as Nicolas explained to what degree his new novel marked not only a departure from but a complete break with his earlier work.

"I wanted this book to be a statement of absolute authenticity, a work that would offer an image of me that is completely fair and accurate, without the slightest artifice or indulgence. An image as authentic as what you see here before you: on one side the peaks of the Esterel mountain range, on the other the Bay of

Angels, with the sea stretching beyond as far as the eye can see. . . ."

It would be unfair to repeat the full extent of Fabry's smug, egotistical revelations, which bordered on parody. As for myself, all I retained was the man's overwhelming desire for redemption. An unconscious desire, no doubt. For what did Nicolas want to be forgiven? For having lived a completely artificial life, dedicated solely to himself and his own aggrandizement. And, I might add, to the destruction of others.

At the stroke of noon I rang the doorbell of Nicolas's apartment on the rue Valois, his most recent indulgence. Everything in my education and background forbade me from calling on people — even close friends — without prior warning.

Nicolas's butler, Emile, answered my ring.

"Good morning, Sir Edward," he said, as if my sudden appearance was the most natural thing in the world. "Mr. Fabry is in the living room."

I made my way down the long hallway. Nicolas, curious as to who had rung, was standing in the doorway.

"Well, well! Edward, what brings you here unannounced?"

"You don't think I was going to fail you in a moment such as this!"

"What a surprise! What a pleasant surprise!" he said, but his tone suggested exactly the contrary. He barely took the trouble to shake my hand before he turned his back, leaving me standing there awkwardly in the hallway, completely taken aback. I remember thinking that Nicolas generally reserved his boorishness for his women. But his lack of manners suited me; I was in no mood for false effusions.

I sauntered into the living room to find Nicolas surrounded by a bevy of women. I noted the presence of his press secretary, whom I already knew, plus several other beauties I had never laid eyes on before. They were all clustered around an enormous television set, chattering like magpies as they watched the end of a news program on some far-distant war about which no one gave a good goddamn. The tall bay windows looked over the well-tended gardens of the Palais-Royal. Colette used to live in this building, I recalled. I wondered if Fabry had bought this apartment with that in mind; perhaps he thought it would further legitimize his literary claims. Or should I say pretensions? In any case, the apartment was imposing, its interior decoration a curious amalgam of a Moscow subway station and the lobby of a major Swiss bank — neo-something-or-other. On one wall was an enormous pink painting signed Klein. The sofas were of white suede; the tables, set very low, were of black lacquer and looked like so many oversize chess pieces judiciously deployed over the black-and-white marble floor.

I enjoyed watching Nicolas move from one square to another, one chess piece to the next, one woman to another, passing out compliments and casting fatal glances in his wake. I didn't have to hear him to know what he was saying; his desperate, overwhelming need to seduce gave him an unerring gift for the right words.

I was sizing up this spectacle when the press secretary suddenly realized I was there. With a professional reflex she threw her arms around me and exclaimed, "Oh, Sir Edward, how delightful to see you!"

Her pleasure seemed sincere, as my unexpected arrival could only be taken as a good omen. I had a considerable reputation as a discoverer of talent, a man with unusual flair for ferreting out manuscripts. That I was on the scene was proof positive that Nicolas would win the Big Prize.

She took my arm and paraded me across the room, into the heart of the storm.

"This is Sir Edward Destry," she trumpeted, "the great English publisher. May I introduce Sabine d'Amecourt from the *Literary Gazette*. And this is Virginia Coretin of *Vogue*. And next to her is Nora Afnazi —"

And my heart began to beat uncontrollably. My eyes were locked on those of the Middle Eastern beauty as though I had been hypnotized. The woman's gestures, her voice, her every movement, held me in thrall. I had the impression that I had seen them before. What distant emotion were they awakening in me? What long-buried memory was her presence unearthing? And yet I had given up any interest in women ages ago. Why was this Nora an exception? I was incapable of saying. My heart was still pounding, out of control. Images and feelings rose in my mind, pell-mell, fleeting and unclear, as in a dream one tries to seize and cannot. Then everything came into focus:

Nora was Yasmina, my Yasmina. The same eyes, the same gentleness, the same savage slenderness.

I could not believe that she was in this room simply by chance; it could only be a sign of fate.

The telephone in the study rang, and Nicolas rushed over to answer, the smile on his face suddenly frozen in a kind of grimace.

Several seconds passed; he looked as if he was going to drop dead, struck down by apoplexy. Then he said matter-of-factly, "I'm on my way." He turned round to the assembled throng. He was pale beneath his summer tan.

"I've got it," he managed in a throaty voice.

His female sycophants rose to their feet as one and buried him beneath a flurry of effusive embraces. Only Nora Afnazi remained serenely seated where she was, refusing to take part. Then she too vanished, with the rest of the harem and the prizewinner himself, whom I had not even had time to congratulate. I stood there alone in front of the television screen. The doors of the Drouant restaurant, where the voting for the Goncourt Prize had taken place, swung open. A dense throng of reporters, photographers, and curious onlookers blocked the exit. Flashes lit up the screen as the photographers vied for the best picture. The president of the jury stepped up to the cluster of microphones and, his eyes blinking in the glare of the lights, announced:

"After eight rounds of voting, this year's Goncourt Prize has been awarded to Nicolas Fabry for —"

The rest of his words were drowned out in the

ensuing uproar. Nicolas and his feminine entourage hurriedly donned raincoats, gathered up umbrellas, and headed out the door.

I had no interest in following them. Emile, perfect and impassive, started to close the doors to the study.

"No, Emile," I said. "Leave the door ajar." Apparently, Emile had not heard my request.

"Emile," I repeated, "ajar, if you please. I would like to see the rest of the television announcement regarding the prize." Actually I had no interest whatsoever in the remaining protocol. I had other plans entirely regarding the study. I switched off the television and headed for Nicolas's study. I took from my briefcase three books yellowed by age and slipped them into the back of the already overloaded top shelf of the enormous bookcases that spanned the wall from floor to ceiling, each between several other books. This graft consisted of three titles: Virginia Woolf's *The Waves*, Clemence Dane's *Legend,* and *The Need to Love* by a certain C. Irving Brown. Then I left the Palais-Royal apartment and walked to Gaillon Square, where the Drouant restaurant was located.

The restaurant was besieged, and Nicolas, who was standing arm-in-arm with his French publisher Laurent Millagard, looked as if he was about to suffocate. But all the earlier emotion was gone. Once again he looked like a blasé conquistador condescending to receive the homage of the tribes he had just vanquished, and he spoke to the journalists with the self-importance of the *Paris Match* interview, evoking his redemption as an author who, as he put it, had been threatened by the very success of his work to date, "not, mind you, that he was turning his back on that body of work, not at all. But with this new book he felt he had managed to attain an important new level as an innovator, a level he had long dreamed of but which till now had eluded him."

He threw everything in but — as the Americans say — the kitchen sink. His life till now, which he described as that of an "inspired nomad"; his "search for truth"; his son, whom he had not had the time to really know; the women in his life, who had loved him and helped guide him toward his cherished goal . . .

"With this book," Fabry went on, "I believe I have given an authentic vision of myself. I would like to stand aside and let the pages of *Il faut aimer* speak for me — what? The size and number of the printings? Of course they're substantial, but I really don't care about that. More than anything, I have a sense of accomplishment, of fulfillment. For the first time in my life I feel in complete accord with my inner self. . . ."

At that point the rain began to fall, slicing through the forest of microphones and scattering the majority of the reporters. Only the truly faithful ignored the watery onslaught and continued hanging on his every word. Fabry held forth for the remaining few as his press secretary tugged on his sleeve.

"Come along, Nicolas, they're waiting for us at the radio station."

They had to shove him into a waiting car to take him to the studios of glory, leaving me alone in the driving rain with his French publisher, drenched to the skin but deliriously happy. He was on cloud nine. It was all I could do to keep him from breaking into song — "Singing in the Rain" would doubtless have been his choice, but at the risk of being a killjoy I said that all this racket had given me a migraine. Yes, yes, I knew I was old-fashioned, from another era, but the fact remained that all this ballyhoo, this media blitz, was abhorrent to me. All of which wasn't very nice of me, I realized, so I tried to make up for it by remarking that this coronation was, after all, the result of our working together for twenty years.

"But this is more than an anniversary," Millagard exclaimed. "This is a crowning achievement, an apotheosis!"

He asked me to join him in his chauffeured car, and as we drove along the banks of the Seine our talk was of how extraordinary a victory this was. We also talked shop, fixing on the date the book would appear in England and agreeing on a figure for the advance that, especially under the circumstances, was completely fair; we had worked too long and hard for this day to argue over such mundane matters. Then, disgusted by the game I was playing, I asked Millagard about the beautiful Nora.

"The little bitch! She has Nicolas wrapped around her little finger."

I found that difficult to believe. "You mean," I suggested, "that unlike the others she doesn't throw herself at his feet." To which Millagard scowled and said, "No, that's not it at all. This is something different. I'd call it role reversal. And if one of the two is going to suffer from the liaison, my crystal ball tells me it will be Fabry." And then, as if to sum it up, he said, nodding sagely, "Black magic, my friend, that's what it is. Black magic."

Or the curse of Yasmina, I thought to myself.

The memory of Nora, whom I had only glimpsed, and with whom I had not exchanged a word, continued to echo in my mind. It brought back painful memories of my past, my youth, my first, my only love. . . .

Chapter 2

"Can you believe it? Ten full minutes on the most-listened-to station in the country! That's more than they gave the Nobel Prize winner! Nicolas was fantastic. A real hit!"

The press secretary didn't realize what she was saying. A hit. True, but the hit was coming from me. And his radio interview just now, and all the newspaper articles that were to follow, all the radio and television coverage, would only tighten the noose around his neck.

The fact was, Fabry's novel was successful beyond his wildest dreams. It was a great book, his only truly major work, the one he had always wanted to write and till now failed to pull off. Fabry, the past master of redundancy, the man who simply could not refrain from preening and primping, had at long last found a tone that was both natural and precise. *Les mots justes,* to paraphrase Flaubert. The right words. He had found them, oh God he had, I realized as soon as I had read the first few pages of the manuscript. And then my surprise turned into a mixture of amazement and rage so overwhelming that I found it hard to breathe. . . .

Remembering all that now, I could feel the anger resurfacing, and I knew I had to banish it from my mind, clear my head completely. If I didn't, I would never be able to keep to plan.

After Nicolas had finished his interview — or should I say performance — at the radio station, where Laurent and I had joined him, the next stop on the glory road was at the publishing house, where a huge cocktail party had been prepared. Everyone who was anyone in the world of letters had been invited.

Laurent and Fabry's press secretary had gone ahead to make sure everything was in order, so it turned out that Nicolas and I were alone in the press secretary's car on the trip to the party. It was the first time we had been alone together since the day several months before when Nicolas had flown to London to deliver me his manuscript. We drove in silence along the Seine, as if embarrassed to be sitting next to each other. Neither of us felt like talking. I knew why I didn't want to. I was hard pressed to understand why Nicolas didn't.

In any case, for once I did not put myself out, and we arrived at the publishing house without exchanging a word.

Nicolas hopped out of the car, leaving me to find a parking space. Not exactly a friendly gesture, I thought, especially since in this part of town parking spaces are at a premium even when there's no party going on. It was a full half hour before I appeared in the overcrowded rooms of the publishing house, where of course Nicolas was surrounded by a mob of reporters. It would be an understatement to say that they were clamoring for his attention.

I stood there for several minutes watching him perform. He was, as always, so wonderfully sure of himself, so colossally overbearing, that my determination to be done with him as soon as possible burned greater than ever.

In truth, have I ever stopped observing him? With admiration, jealousy, or hate? For years that fascination nourished my own self-disgust, that *Selbsthass* — self-hatred — that I wore like a hair shirt. Today I hate myself less, doubtless because I hate him more. The women's press were crowding around him now, their tones if anything more strident than those of their male colleagues. With them Nicolas was pompous, smooth, and to my mind slightly ridiculous. God, what bombast to respond to one stupid question after another — always the same ones, it seemed to me — the women were shouting at him.

"The kind of women I prefer? Oh, good Lord, how can I answer that one? Every woman to whom I find myself attracted possesses a particle of the universal grace that touches me to the very depths of my soul. . . . What after all is seduction if not that strange power of fascination for the inaccessible body, so close, when all is said and done, that one can only properly refer to it as God? Yes, God. Why not? . . .

"Do I sleep in the nude? . . . As a matter of fact, I do. Why? Perhaps a simple desire to return to the basic state of nature, or perhaps in keeping with the nomadic impulse I feel so strongly within me . . .

"No, adultery in my work is never a simple aberration of the body in search of its own truth. . . .

"Please, my friends, give me a little room, if you don't mind. . . ."

He would have gone on forever with his shameless striptease if Christiane, Millagard's wife, had not suddenly called for silence. She strode over to Nicolas, smiling broadly, and handed a cordless phone to him.

"It's Peter," she announced.

"Oh, Peter! What a nice surprise!"

The red light on the television camera clicked on, and once again microphones were pushed toward Fabry to catch this touching spectacle of the father talking to his beloved son, who was in a Swiss boarding school and therefore unable to be with his father on this day of days.

Dear Peter, my godson, I could picture him on the other side of the Alps, in the exclusive school to which his father had banished him since he had divorced the boy's mother. Nicolas would never admit it, but this too-handsome, too-blond boy was a constant reminder of this failure in his life, and Nicolas hated to lose. In his ultra-chic school Peter no doubt rubbed elbows with Saudi princes and the sons of billionaires from around the world, but neither the gilded youth around him nor the welcoming ski slopes of Gstaad had ever been able to compensate for the fact that his parents had abandoned him. I lavished as much affection on him as I could, and at this point I loved him like a father. I believe, in fact, that he loved me more than he did his own father, which, it goes without saying, infuriated Fabry.

The love duo over the phone had gone on for about two minutes when Nicolas erupted with a series of exclamations that were like an avalanche roaring down the mountains into the valley.

"What's that? My check hasn't arrived? But they should have called and told me! What? It was Edward who paid? Why in the hell didn't you let me know sooner, you little jerk!"

The father-son dialogue, artfully staged by Millagard's wife to show the human side of Fabry, was fast turning sour. Suddenly Nicolas was seen as perhaps not quite the model father he had made himself out to be. Not only that, but anyone who wanted to could read into his remarks that despite his fame and fortune he was niggardly in paying for his own son's boarding school. Not exactly the kind of image he wanted to send out into the world.

From that moment on, the reporters' questions became increasingly insidious. They began to focus more and more on his personal life. Since you love your son so much, Mr. Fabry, could you explain why you didn't keep him with you after the divorce? Yes, and about the divorce: is it final now? Mr. Fabry, Mr. Fabry, is there any truth to the rumor that your ex-wife tried to commit suicide?

The party was turning into a slaughter, and Nicolas was clearly floundering, tangled up in explanations and self-justifications. It was all Millagard's wife could do to extricate him from the disaster. At that point I felt disgust for the whole spectacle; all those high-and-mighty, gossipy Parisian intellectuals. The buffet tables, now stripped of their offerings, looked for all the world like some glorified garbage dump. The whole place had the sorry look of the day after a major party. But the party wasn't over. It was simply moving on to Castel's restaurant, where dinner was being served for close friends and colleagues only.

Needless to say, I was one of the happy few.

Can one ever suppress remorse?

That night, faced with the radiant joy of my old, esteemed colleague Millagard, I thought I was never going to pull it off. I had never seen Millagard in a better mood, more expansive, more confident, trumpeting to one and all that I was the best, the greatest publisher in England. Twice in the course of the evening he hugged me and said, "I'm so happy to see you, Edward I can't tell you how happy. What we're celebrating tonight is our work. Our joint efforts —"

And I knew that very shortly I was going to hurt this man, this good and decent man with whom I had worked closely for so many years, that I was going to make him not only suffer but suffer horribly. I felt a surge of shame rise within me. And for a moment I came within a hair of doing an about-face, turning off the hellish machine that I had set in motion. Nothing would have been easier.

But at that moment Nicolas arrived at the restaurant with Nora Afnazi on his arm. A burst of applause greeted him, igniting my hate all over again. He had regained his self-assurance, which had faltered in the wake of the phone conversation with his son, and he responded to the invited guests with that condescending smile that so exasperated me. I noted too that he studiously avoided making eye contact with me, as if the few thousand Swiss francs I had paid to his son's boarding school was an embarrassment to him. He sat down at the far end of the table, and immediately a ballet of waiters began swirling about us.

Nora . . . Yasmina . . . my love stolen by this sleight-of-hand artist. This seducer. How lovely she was, this reincarnation of the only woman I had ever loved! And there she was, seated on Nicolas's right, whereas on my right sat a two-hundred-pound-plus collection of soft, undulating flesh, belonging to a woman well into her forties who, when she spoke, did not talk but thundered, a woman whose makeup was at its thinnest a good inch thick, and whose arm bracelets rang as loudly as the bells of Westminster Abbey. Ah, yes, Margot Zembla, the high priestess of French literary critics. I knew little about her except that her tongue was razor sharp, much given to cutting, and frequently to murdering, her literary victims. Seeing her here was enough to convince me that the reputation that preceded her was indeed based on fact.

Leaning out over her plate, she was gorging herself, eating out loud, with moving mandibles more than audible. She was one of those rare creatures gifted with the capacity to chew and enunciate at the same time. Thus, still chewing away, she told me how highly she thought of Nicolas's novel. "A revelation," she said, a true bovine, except that her cud was a mouthful of caviar. "And believe me, I know genius when I see it."

She had the thick, scratchy voice of a woman who smoked as heartily as she ate.

Hardly believing my eyes, I watched her devour half of the appetizers at our end of the table, followed by two brook trout, plus a filet of duck. Then, seeing I still had not done justice to my duck, she reached across and planted her fork in it, as if she were planting her flag to take possession of a conquered foreign country.

"You're not eating that?" she said, her mouth still full.

And without waiting for my reply she gulped down what was left on my plate in two generous mouthfuls. That amazing voracity, which had initially disgusted me, suddenly became fascinating.

"I hope you don't find me too gluttonous," the ogress simpered.

No, in a curious way she made me hungry, and when I told her so she seemed touched in the depths of her distant soul. She began to hang on my every word, her eyes fixed on mine, her jaws working away without respite, the better to please me no doubt. Her oversize, insatiable mouth, her fat thigh rubbing lightly against mine, her enormous breasts, which hung out over the table, made me slightly ill and aroused at the same time. If I kept piling food on her plate each time it was empty, it was more to turn me on than to satisfy her ravenous appetite, for my desire was an ambiguous mixture of wanting to possess her on the one hand and hurt myself on the other.

I began drinking, to protect myself from the swirling eddies into which she was taking me, to drown my remorse, and to fan the fires of my hatred for Nicolas. I kept trying to catch his eye, but each time I did he made a point of looking the other way. A premonition?

When the "chef's surprise" arrived on the table — a multitiered cake crowned with a quill pen of sugar — there was a new round of applause, and the guests began chanting for the laureate — who asked for nothing more — to make a speech. He pushed back his chair, rose to his feet, and with his best Jimmy Stewart — "modesty is my name" — recalled ingratiatingly, in case those present might not have thought of it, that he had had to wait for thirty years to win the coveted Goncourt Prize, whereas any number of lesser writers, whose names the present company would be hard pressed to remember today, had won it before him.

"For an ex-diplomat," chortled my next-door glutton, "tact does not exactly seem to be his strong suit, does it?"

Then Fabry took off into the philosophical wild blue yonder, somewhere just this side of the sublime but closer to the ridiculous, a witches' brew of empty words, unbearable phonemes, and jumbled redundancies, winging back to earth with this infuriating conclusion:

"The colors of the Middle East have taken possession of my pen once and for all. Everything I have written up to now strikes me as pale and lifeless. I was walking alone in a wasteland, transparent, like a ghost, leaving no trace in my wake, reduced to nothing more than a gaze in the empty space through which I passed. From now on I am like a child who has just received his first set of watercolors. In my other books — and this is not to say I am turning my back on them — I was applying the primer, the undercoat, for all my future work —"

I mean really! The man should have been brought to trial and locked up on the charge of flagrant self-conceit.

With those closing words he bid the assembled throng good night and withdrew with all the pomp and dignity befitting his new station, taking the lovely Nora with him.

Their departure sounded the death knell of the evening's festivities. In any case we were more or less drunk, and I was running a high fever, a kind of erotic fever brought on by the bestial bulimia of Margot Zembla. Thus I politely declined Millagard's invitation to drive me back to my hotel. We departed with a warm embrace, agreeing to meet the next day for lunch before I took my plane back to London.

I had taken no more than a dozen steps down the rue Princesse when my ogress caught up with me and grabbed my arm. With her hair like a nest of infuriated vipers, she conjured up one of those Gorgons who hunted down humans, creatures who are the reflection of their guilt, the deformed image of themselves. Those

23

who had the misfortune to look upon them were, if memory served, turned to stone. But for me, this fateful day, I looked upon her as heaven-sent, an ambassador of destiny, come to shame me but also to deliver me from a fate that had so long held me prisoner.

Another wink from the eye of fate: my hotel bar was closed, which meant that I had no choice but to offer my Medusa a nightcap in the intimacy of my room. Offer made, offer accepted.

I had not slept with a woman for thirty years. Not since the death of my beloved Yasmina. Castrated by sorrow. Castrated by guilt as well.

And now Margot Zembla was playing the unwitting role of exorcist. The unlikely combination of her sexual bulimia, the depraved poses she insisted on striking, and her verbal obscenity did the job, and I soon found myself fully aroused. Sullying myself against her skin, I took the first steps toward curing myself, and like a man possessed, in a fit of diabolical madness, of morbid hallucination, I took her once, twice, and then again, and each time it was Nicolas I was destroying beneath me.

Finally she fell into a deep sleep, accompanied by sounds not unlike those of a sink being unblocked. Her snoring in itself was enough to have sounded the retreat of the most romantic love story in history. I offered these nocturnal noises up as a sacrifice, a burnt offering. They were part and parcel of my punishment. I didn't sleep a wink all night, exorcised to be sure but disgusted as well, disgusted with myself and with this body sprawled next to me.

I fell asleep at the precise moment when the

telephone rang. It was eight o'clock, and the noise-prone object of my desires ended her nightlong pipe-emptying labors and, opening her booze-reddened eyes, gazed longingly upon me.

I drank the cup to the dregs. When breakfast was served she insisted on eating it not only in bed but naked in bed. Or, rather, naked on the bed. I looked in awe as she wolfed down her breakfast, in her own simpering, gourmand manner. Nor did I turn away when she struggled into her dress, repacked her gelatinous flesh into her orange suit. I listened to the gargantuan gargling noises that later emanated from the bathroom. All part of my atonement, to be sure, but also because I sensed that one day Fat Margot would be useful to me, would become an integral part of my plan. One day in the not too distant future, our paths would cross again.

"The next time I'm in Paris," I said, always the gentleman, as I escorted her to the door, "I trust I can ring you up for dinner."

After a long, hot shower I felt better. I called my office and told my faithful secretary, Doris — whom the staff referred to as "High Fidelity" behind her back — that I was returning on the next plane. The trying night I had just gone through had eliminated any desire I might have had to lunch with Millagard. I rang him and begged off, on the pretense that some urgent matter had just come up and I had to fly immediately back to London.

In the plane I leafed through the Paris newspapers. The *Figaro* carried a story about the Goncourt on the front page, but the article was relatively short. A brief biography of Fabry, plus a few lines about the ceremony itself at Drouant's and the reception that followed at the publishing house. No mention at all of the conversation between Peter and his father. That kind of thing would take a while to seep down, turn into gossip, and be picked up by the scandal sheets. If my intuition proved right, the kick-off would come from none other than my obscene conquest of the previous night.

And then all of a sudden I felt oddly ill at ease. I felt emptied, dizzy, chilled to the marrow of my bones. This last confrontation with Nicolas had done me in. When I had set off to see him in Paris, I had hoped — I had hoped for what, really? That he greet me with a roll of drums and a flourish of trumpets? Like his old friend, without whom he could not operate? Sir Edward the indispensable? Perhaps. And what if he had greeted me in that way, with warmth and affection? Would I have been moved? Enough to switch off the revenge machine?

I doubt it. In any case, I felt that I had once again been made to play the fool. For how many years now had my blind devotion filled the bottomless pit of his conceit? To him it had always appeared perfectly normal that I be the servant of his destiny.

During all those long years when he held me in thrall, I had always felt ashamed of myself. Nicolas had been in the limelight. I had remained in the shadows. The way it had been in Alexandria.

Chapter 3

Alexandria, Egypt, thirty-five years earlier.

"Edward, my boy, you must learn to be more sociable. You really must. Are you telling me that you don't even have one friend here?"

"No, Mom, I don't," I grunted, affecting the frightful American accent that so exasperated my mother.

And it was true. I fled the company of the English boys my own age, who I found to be a bunch of snobs, hopelessly trivial and hatefully arrogant. God had created me both shy and unsociable, and I preferred reading the banned poets to bowing and scraping to my elders and compatriots in the course of some hoity-toity evening. I enjoyed diving into the waves of Stanley Bay and swimming until I was exhausted, or exploring the labyrinths of the Kom el-Chugafa catacombs, much more than showing off in front of some well-brought-up young ladies.

Whether my mother liked it or not, my only

friends were Elias Zarani, the son of a Jewish shop-keeper from Syria, and Irene Pastrodis, the daughter of a Greek pastry chef. It goes without saying that they were not suitable company for the yearly ball held at the Alexandria Country Club. For while all the ethnic groups in the Tower of Babel called Alexandria lived and worked together in peace and harmony, they also knew how to avoid one another, usually in accordance with very simple rules, of which money was the major factor.

Elias, Irene, and I formed an inseparable trio, united by the common bond of literature, and the three of us had managed to found a small literary magazine, which we baptized the *Middle Eastern Review.* In its pages we published the work of Egyptian poets, which we translated ourselves, plus of course our own adolescent poetic efforts. Although the magazine appeared irregularly, we had a proud total of one hundred subscribers. Our editorial board meetings took place anywhere we chose to hold them, preferably at the beach or even, at times, in the Mediterranean itself. None of which prevented us from maintaining the most rigorous literary standards. When you are eighteen, tolerance is not your prime quality.

So it was that I went to the country club dance alone — or, to be more precise, chaperoned by my mother. She doubtless was hoping against hope that in the course of the evening I would meet the girl of my dreams — a pretty, well-brought-up English girl, of course — who would both bring me happiness and do honor to our family. And, to tell the truth, I was pleased to have come, if only to savor the beauty of the warm, lively summer night, lit by a constellation of torches and sumptuous fireworks. To bathe in the odor of jasmine and carob, odors of luxury married to those of misery. From one end of the city to the other, Alexandria assaults the senses with this contrast of smells.

It was a formal ball, with just the right mixture of tall, flat-chested English girls, wealthy Egyptian young ladies, and younger siblings and cousins from both groups who seemed to spend most of the evening blushing. I could doubtless have found my true love among them, but I was a poor dancer, and not one to make much of an effort on the social front.

I remember that I was watching with fascination as a girl who weighed roughly twice what she should have twisted and turned on the dance floor, moving her buttocks in a circular motion like a gigantic spinning top, when I saw him.

He was crossing the dance floor at a steady, determined pace, heading directly for our table, and he kept his eyes locked on mine. I had the impression that the air parted on both sides to make way for him. It was beauty — pure, all-conquering beauty — coming toward me, holding out his hand for me to shake, smiling, introducing himself:

"Nicolas Fabry. I have just arrived here from Paris with my father. He's the new French consul general in Alexandria."

He had the voice of a cello.

"Edward Destry," I managed; but, I thought there must be a mistake, a creature this handsome could not have been looking for me. But no, I was wrong, it was indeed me he had been looking for, or rather the editor of the *Middle Eastern Review* he wanted to congratulate. "For my admirable work," was the way he put it.

"Thank you . . . ah . . . thank you very much," I stammered, sincerely flattered to have a new reader — our one hundred and first — and unsettled that it was he, this creature of light.

He sat down beside me, and I was ready to do his bidding, whatever it might have been. He wrote prose, I thought I heard him saying. "What a coincidence," I heard myself responding, "That is precisely what I'm looking for in the magazine." He would like very much to work with me? Of course, of course. Right now, if that suited him. From the minute I laid eyes on him I was enslaved.

Dawn was beginning to cast its first faint light on the veranda of the club, and Nicolas and I were still in deep discussion. We had run through the gamut of contemporary literature, the way generals review their troops, in minute detail. He was familiar with all the major French writers, and his pronouncements about their work had the finality of a judge passing sentence. I was impressed. We then moved on to the *Middle Eastern Review,* and I listened to his criticism of our valiant efforts. In fact, he was murdering the magazine. His barbed comments were so many banderillas thrust into the beast, and blood was oozing from the wounds. He even demolished a poem by my dear friend Elias, and I was furious with myself at not finding the courage to defend him. The problem was, I loved his poetry far too much to feel it needed to be defended.

Did Nicolas realize that he had gone too far? In

any case, he abruptly loosened the intellectual vise in which he had held me captive for several hours and proposed we go look at the sunrise.

Delighted, I suggested we go to the old fort of Kait-Bey on Pharos Island. He thought that was a splendid idea, and on our way out of the club he rounded up a dozen or so young members to join us. Everyone managed to squeeze into the limousine that was standing in front of the club entrance, awaiting Nicolas's orders. The driver was fast asleep at the wheel, snoring away peacefully, until an authoritative tap on his shoulder by young Nicolas startled him awake.

"To the old fort," Nicolas barked.

Literature had now been relegated to the background; the *Middle Eastern Review* was no longer a subject worthy of conversation. Nicolas was on to other things, and within minutes I discovered a whole other person, Nicolas-the-Seducer, Nicolas as Lovelace, the lady's man for whom, even at that tender age, the code of love held no secrets. My shyness had always kept me from even striking up a conversation with the lovely Nathalie Lherbier, whom I had nonetheless ogled from afar for many years. And here was Nicolas, who had known her for a scant ten minutes, holding her in his arms and whispering sweet nothings into her ear as she let her head loll placidly on his shoulder.

Once we were on the island, he focused solely on her. He put his arm around her waist, ostensibly to help her clamber over the scattered blocks of stone that lay along the path to the fort, while I played the role of guide, conjuring up the gun salutes of the British navy, the majestic beauty of this soaring white-marble tower from which, in times past, burned a fire visible from great distances in all directions. I declaimed about the special sound of the waves crashing on the walls of the fort, and to show off to Nicolas, I went so far as to recite the poem by el-Deraui that I had translated into English:

> From its lofty platform
> I thought that the sea below me
> Was a cloud,
> And thence I saw my friends
> Like stars. . . .

My friends were shivering in their scanty gala frocks, and I could see that Nicolas was unimpressed by my poem. He was too busy kissing Nathalie. Together on a granite monolith, itself the color of sunrise, they looked in dawn's early light like the Dioscuri, the twin sons of the god of light to which the lighthouse of Alexandria had been dedicated two thousand years before. As for me, I no longer existed. In a single evening Nicolas had conquered and rejected me. I suddenly was overcome by a terrible feeling of loneliness, of having been unfairly banished. And a wound opened within me that would never heal.

How can I describe it? From that time on I began to create a vacuum within myself, to abdicate my personality to make room for Nicolas's wishes and desires.

He wanted me to go with him to this place or that? I managed to extricate myself from whatever obligation I might have had. Of course I was free. He called the roll, and I responded "present and accounted for" each time, proud that he should need me. I devoted myself to his every caprice with the pride of modesty, overwhelmed that someone so superior could take an interest in someone like me. When you are young you need role models. Finding nothing lovable about myself, I transferred my love to him. I built an altar to him. Perhaps he, for his part, dreamed of having a slave to validate his authority.

It is pointless to say how excited I was about introducing my newfound idol to my friends Elias and Irene.

The encounter took place during the first days of warm weather. To celebrate the arrival of spring, we organized an elaborate picnic on the banks of Lake Mariout, in a tiny oasis on the edge of the desert. I had borrowed my parents' Land Rover. Nicolas had pressed into service the French consulate's cook, Mohammad. Elias had brought the lamb, which was to be roasted on a spit, and Irene had taken care of the wine: a bottle of Clos Mariout — a dry white wine — and two bottles of a wonderful Matamir red, a kind of Chateau Margaux from the banks of the Nile. The recent rains had covered the dunes with multicolored flowers, miraculous but ephemeral blankets of pink and white, foreshadowing the fate of all the young men who, in the nearby desert, would soon give up their lives.

But the cadence of marching boots, the Munich

conference that would soon decide the fate of so many, meant little or nothing to us then. The heads of state could sign any pacts they wanted, we couldn't have cared less.

The roast lamb was superb. The wines were a work of art. And yet the picnic was a total disaster; I could tell that Elias and Irene could not bear my new friend. Nicolas was the principal culprit, for he showed off shamelessly. Instead of dazzling us, he bored and irritated us with his literary name dropping and smug opinions. I was more than slightly embarrassed for him, and in an effort to make amends I kept filling up everyone's glass the minute it was empty. I cracked jokes till my face hurt. All I wanted, more than anything in the world, was that we all like one other!

I especially wanted us all to be friends because, the night before, Nicolas had brought me a short story that he had written in English entitled, "The Life Before Us." I had virtually promised that it would appear in the next issue of the magazine, without having read it — an act of faith.

Faith misplaced; it was a shameless plagiarism of Raymond Radiguet's *Devil in the Flesh*. So shameless in fact that in this brief, truncated version whole passages had been lifted from Radiguet's original, word for word. How could Nicolas have been so blatant? I hadn't found the courage to tell him that his text was not only worthless but scandalous to boot. In reworking the story, I convinced myself, I could camouflage the plagiarism and make the story acceptable to Elias and Irene. Wrong again!

Back in Alexandria, after the disastrous picnic, I

set about reworking Nicolas's story from A to Z, blue-penciling the stolen passages. But even in its edited version the story remained a pathetic pastiche. Irene declared that it would appear in the magazine over her dead body. Elias added that the story had no place in our review anyway, since there was nothing Middle Eastern about it. I chose the worst of all possible solutions: I changed the layout of the magazine and inserted Nicolas's story without telling the others. The next day I secretly went with the manuscript pages of the new issue to our Armenian printer, a man named Papazian.

Normally Papazian greeted me with open arms. A man of considerable culture, he was in the habit of discussing Egyptian poetry with me, usually at great length. I discovered a multitude of poetic treasures each time I went to see him. Thanks to him, the *Middle Eastern Review* had published a number of texts of extraordinary quality and beauty, of which even the major literary reviews of England and the Continent had no awareness.

But this time Papazian did not greet me with his usual warmth. Without raising his eyes from his typesetting machine, he asked me coldly to put the manuscript on the table. It was his way of saying that he would appreciate my paying him the fifty pounds sterling that I had owed him for several months now. I had kept Elias and Irene in the dark about the debt, feeling it was my obligation to take care of it by God knows what miracle. Today, however, I vowed to pay Papazian within the week.

"What!" Nicolas said when he learned of my

embarrassment, "Why didn't you tell me?" And he pulled from his pocket a thick wad of bills that he put on the table.

"Will this take care of it?" he said.

"But," I stammered, "I . . . I didn't ask you for the money."

Still, I ended up accepting it. I was enormously grateful for his immediate display of generosity, and moved as well by his next words.

"The *Middle Eastern Review* has got to be saved," he said emphatically. "Ridiculous that it should go under for such a paltry sum. As long as I'm around —"

By God, I thought, for all his posturing, here's a friend who puts his money where his mouth is. Now, to some degree, the magazine was his. All three of us were indebted to him. But I, naive as I was, hadn't thought that one through at the time.

I hate to recall the day when this accursed issue of the magazine appeared. It sounded the death knell of the great friendship that had bound Elias, Irene, and me together. For over thirty years now, whenever I hark back to that day, my heart is filled with shame.

I can still remember vividly the icy welcome I received when I showed up at the Pastrodis pastry shop, where we usually met to celebrate the publication of each new issue. No celebration that day. No multicolored pastries, no raki to wash them down. Only a cup of Turkish coffee, the powdery dregs of which had already dried on the edges of the glasses. I sat down at the table, expecting the worst. It was Irene who fired the first salvo.

"Why in the world did you do that?" Her tone was below freezing.

"I couldn't help it," I said lamely.

"Would you mind letting us in on your little secret?" Elias chimed in.

"I would have much preferred to have kept you in the dark," I began. "But I owe you the truth, the whole truth. You may not know it, but the magazine owes a great deal of money to the printer."

And I launched into a long, rambling explanation. Instead of admitting that I was completely under the spell of Nicolas, I got tangled up in all sorts of vague and untenable justifications. I made a sorry effort to explain how, because the magazine was ridden with debt, I had allowed Nicolas to bail me out. How then could I refuse to publish his story?

They didn't believe a word of it. Worse, they were in no mood to forgive me.

"Since you want to give the magazine a new tone," Elias declared, "you can consider that we are no longer involved. We leave the baby in your hands. The only thing I can say is that I hope you don't sink any lower than you already have. . . . Oh, and give our best to your new mentor."

They left the shop without even shaking hands. I remained seated there, completely devastated. I had stupidly offered up my best friends as a sacrifice to Nicolas's machinations. My only friends, actually. I can still hear the hum of the ceiling fan turning lazily above my head in the pastry shop, stirring my sorrow.

The rest of the day was just as dreadful. As I was leaving Pastrodis's shop, my eyes red from the tears I couldn't hold back after Elias and Irene had deserted me, who should I run into but Nicolas? If that wasn't bad enough, he had on his arm his current conquest, another of the superb young ladies from school whom I'd been eyeing from afar for several years but never had the courage to speak to. Her name was Jeanne Brisson, and her extraordinary green eyes had already turned more than a few heads in the city despite her tender age.

Nicolas could see how upset I was and rushed over to me, exclaiming, "What's wrong, Edward? Tell me what's bothering you."

I could have killed him. I told him that I was suffering from an eye infection and threw in some other pathetic excuse for my sorry state. Then, forcing a smile, I pulled from my briefcase a copy of the new issue of the *Middle Eastern Review* and handed it to him.

"What's that you have there?" he asked with feigned astonishment.

"You know very well. It's the new issue of the magazine. Take a look at page three, you'll find a story that's very — anyway, a text you're familiar with."

I couldn't help but admire the restraint he displayed in what had to be an important moment in his young life, seeing his name in print for the first time. But he was too much in control of his emotions — assuming he had any to control — to show the slightest pleasure, even if it was narcissistic. Jeanne Brisson was looking at the magazine over his shoulder.

"Well, well," Nicolas murmured, acting as if he were surprised. "I see someone has been rummaging through my wastebasket. Could it have been you, my dear Edward?"

"But that's the story you submitted to me, as you well —"

"Don't be ridiculous," he cut me off. "Completely ridiculous. I wrote that when I was fifteen. You could at least have had the courtesy to ask my permission before publishing it!"

"But I thought that . . . You told me that . . ."

"Please, Edward!"

That was the final blow. I should have reacted then and there. Protested, lost my temper, told him off in no uncertain terms. Because of him I had just lost my two best friends. Because of him I had been caught off guard in the street, completely distraught. And he'd had the gall to act indignant, simply to show off in front of Miss Brisson! Even worse, he had pretended as he glanced at the story not to notice that I had rewritten it for him to eliminate all the embarrassing plagiarisms. . . .

Like a beaten dog, I slunk away, my tail between my legs, more miserable than I had ever been in my life. The sad fact was, I had been completely incapable of standing up for myself.

The following issue of the *Middle Eastern Review* appeared less than two months later. Till then, I had been in charge of ferreting out potentially publishable material and making the initial selection, which I would then submit to my "editorial board." But in the new setup Nicolas would determine the table of contents all by himself. Need I add that most of the new magazine's contents were the work of one Nicolas Fabry? My efforts consisted chiefly of rewriting his texts, under the guise of smoothing out his English, which was less than perfect. In exchange, I had the right to "include" some of my own work. If I put that word in quotes it is because it was the very word Nicolas used, to make it clear that it was only through my role as managing editor that this rare privilege was granted me. In other words, my work would never have made it into the magazine on its own merits.

Under these circumstances, I simply turned over the magazine to Nicolas to do with as he wished. He soon grew weary of it, and the *Middle Eastern Review* passed quietly into history.

Chapter 4

Having given up the magazine, I sought refuge more and more frequently in the catacombs of Kom el-Chugafa, on the Hill of Tiles. It was my refuge.

I felt safe here, far from the harsh real world, far from the sounds of the war that had just broken out back in Europe. Denmark and Norway had been invaded and conquered, and Hitler was pursuing his pre-ordained path of conquest. Most of the tourists in Egypt had decided they had better cut short their visit and return home, leaving me virtually the sole master of this underground archaeological marvel.

As I descended the circular staircase, flanked with hand-carved niches and graves, I left all my worldly worries and sorrows behind. In the main room of the catacombs, with its funereal beds carved into the rocks on all sides, I felt completely at peace. A faint light illuminated the walls, making the Gorgon masks, the Roman caduceuses, and the obelisks of the pharoahs come alive, pulling me back into the past. I could have stayed there for hours, seated on my bed of stone, lost in my thoughts, dreaming of times long gone, until Mansour, the guardian, arrived to announce by tapping on the glass casing that it was closing time. Then it was a real struggle for me to wrench myself away from my idle forays through history and force myself back into the twentieth century.

Although we had not had more than a dozen exchanges in the year that I had been coming here, Mansour and I had become good friends. He was an authentic bedouin chief, who had been chased out of the Libyan desert by the approach of the war. He and his whole retinue — which included several wives and God knows how many children — had sought refuge here in Egypt, where they barely managed to keep body and soul together, thanks mainly to his post as guardian of the catacombs. Once he had invited me into his "home" — little more than a shanty pieced together with wood and tin — to share with him the ritual glass of mint tea that bedouin chiefs offer their honored guests.

One day, upon arriving at the catacombs, I found to my surprise that Mansour was not at his accustomed post. Curious, I walked over to the large, triangular tent that housed his many children, to be greeted by a wild-looking young girl with gray-green, almond-shaped eyes. She was barefoot, and on her face — forehead, nose, and cheeks — were the delicate blue tattoos common to all bedouins.

She was dark-skinned and lively, like the half-wild goats that were part of Mansour's retinue, and she was dressed more in rags than in what one could call clothes.

"Where is Mansour?" I asked her in Arab.

"My father is feeling ill."

"What's the matter with him? Nothing serious, I trust."

"The heart," she murmured, thrusting her hand through her rags onto her left breast.

"A heart attack!" I exclaimed, genuinely upset.

"Both things," she said.

"What do you mean, both things? Could you be clearer?"

"The heart and the vagabond soul. His heart was choking. But his soul is ill as well."

"Is he in the hospital?"

"Yes, since yesterday. But he gave me the keys."

She unlocked the catacomb doors, then disappeared.

Seated on my stone bench in the banquet hall, I was dreaming of the pagan ceremonies that had taken place there between the lighted columns, opposite the two Anubises, the gods whose task it was to care for the dead, the gods who are lords of the necropolis. . . .

I was daydreaming, trying to imagine where those who died wandered before they reached the Valley of the Immortals.

A high-pitched laugh responded to my silent question. A laugh that echoed throughout the vaulted ceiling. And suddenly I saw her, only a few steps away from me, in her tattered dress. It was a strange apparition. I blinked my eyes.

"What are you doing here?" I asked, taken aback by her sudden arrival.

"But I've come to see you, Destry *effendi*," she said, hastening to add, "I learned your name from my father."

"Would you care to have a seat?"

She spun around, the way a ballerina would, then sat down on the bench beside me. She laughed again, and her mischievous eyes stared boldly at mine.

"I've been watching you for a long time," she said. "My name is Yasmina."

"How old are you?" I asked her, more for something to say than because I really cared.

"Sixteen."

I knew she was lying. She couldn't have been more than fourteen, but I could sense that she was no longer a child.

"You're lying."

She reached over and pinched my lips with her thumb and finger, as if to tell me to hush. It was at that point that I must have made a strenuous effort to leave my historical daydreams behind and move back to my own era. She put her arms around my neck, and I rocked back onto the stone bench. Her mouth locked onto mine, and her tongue began to play over my lips ever so lightly, then moved onto my cheeks. Her hands, stained with henna, circled my body like will-o'-the-wisps in the semidarkness. She hugged me tightly, then opened the buttons of my shirt and snuggled against my chest. I didn't know how to respond.

It wasn't as if I didn't know what it was all about. I had lost my virginity years ago. My school friends and I had made our share of visits to the local whorehouse. But the gallant whores of our fair city, overworked by the hordes of soldiers who lined up for their services, were not of a sort to make young men dream romantic dreams. In fact, my sexual experiences had been purely mechanical. Never before had I felt anything remotely like what I was feeling now, this vertigo, this total sensual abandonment. Yasmina was doing things to me that I had never felt before, and suddenly I desired her. Wildly. Now. Nothing existed in me except this overwhelming need to take her. I ripped off her rags, lay her down beneath me on the bed of stone, slipped my hand between her thighs and possessed her, without the least precaution. I was overcome by an enormous wave that welled up within me and filled my entire being, so strong that I felt my body trembling with desire from head to toe. And at the same time I heard her scream in pain. It was then that I realized Yasmina was a virgin.

I fell in love with her on the spot. Hopelessly in love. Her name was on my lips a hundred times a day, raced endlessly through my head. Yasmina . . . Yasmina . . . I kept saying it out loud over and over again. When I wasn't with her I spent all my time waiting for us to be together again. I loved to death this creature who had appeared out of nowhere. My nerves were constantly on edge, my blood was churning. I suffered and reveled in my suffering, savoring the first fruits of love before she reappeared. My heart was on fire. Yes, I know that's a frightful cliché, but that's how it was. I would arrive with my arms filled with sweets; I would embrace her, kiss her madly, completely out of control, and we would spend several hours making love on the old blanket I had sneaked out of the house.

As soon as her father was back on his feet we had to abandon the banquet hall and find other secret places to make love, for the few tourists who were still in Egypt might have surprised us in the act now that Yasmina no longer was the keeper of the keys. The underground ruins of the ancient pharaohs provided us with a thousand possibilities, and we ended up choosing a little chapel that one could lock with a key as the site of our amorous exploits, with only the Ptolemaic gods who adorned the walls as our witnesses.

To keep Mansour from becoming suspicious, I continued to pay weekly visits to the banquet hall of the catacombs, where I presumably would continue dreaming of times past. The ritual remained unchanged, the only difference being that my visits became shorter and shorter, and as for the content of my daydreams, their only subject was Yasmina. Sometimes I was overcome with doubt. I imagined that perhaps she did not really love me, that the only reason she had given herself to me was to escape the narrow world of her douar. Once, she had told me, her father took her with him to the fashionable streets of the big city, and she was dazzled by the bright lights, the stores, the markets, and the thousand and one temptations that beckoned wherever you looked. She was dying to escape her desert life. There was no way, she once said, that she was going to settle for the fate of generations of women before her, to live out her life in a bedouin tent: an arranged marriage, pregnancies one after the other, exhausting, never-ending labors.

She also had no illusion that flaunting her charms would lead her to the paradise that she envisioned. She knew it wouldn't.

Still, I sometimes had nightmares that she would in fact sell herself to the highest bidder, and when I imagined it I suffered the pangs of absolute hell. But the minute I saw her arrive, I chased the very notion from my mind. I was there, ready and willing to save her from her fate. I still believed that love was forever, and I vaguely understood that I could never love another woman.

We spent every day of that enchanted summer together, and each day was a blessing renewed. No sadness except for my fears ever cast the slightest cloud over us in these months we spent together. We made plans for the future. The world was this chapel in which, like a raging torrent, we made love over and over again. I lived only for love, and when I left her, I prolonged our time together by reliving every minute of the hours just past, continuing to revel in the wonders of her body, her caresses, the way she looked at me while we were making love.

Everything that stood between us — age, race, station — was as nothing, so great, so undying was my love.

And then one day Yasmina failed to appear at the appointed hour, and I learned the agony of waiting. I did my best to reassure myself, conjuring up all sorts of reasons why she couldn't come. And yet I returned home in a terrible state: I was sad, disappointed, and extremely worried. The next day I literally ran to Kom el-Chugafa. Again I waited for her in vain, pacing back and forth in the funeral chapel, listening for the slightest sound from the labyrinth, rushing toward the spiral staircase when I heard, or thought I heard, someone coming, then lying down on the stone and trying to fall asleep, in the vain hope that she would wake me up with a kiss.

Four long days went by in this way. It was only the following Saturday that I saw her again, and I immediately knew that something had changed. Her smile was different, her eyes were sad. She was slipping away from me, and I needed her so much. Too much. I could not imagine that there could be an end to our happiness. That day I made love to her with a tenderness tinged with fear, and when it was over I did not hear the mischievous laugh that I had learned to love so much.

She gently explained to me that her father had found her a job as a maid working for some Europeans, and therefore we would not be able to see each other as often as we had. In fact, only one day a week, Saturday, and she wasn't even sure about that. Her employers were very demanding, she said. Her hours were long and she was seldom let out of the house. She refused to tell me who they were or where they lived. She gave me a brief parting kiss, then said she would see me at the same time the following Saturday.

For two long months I lived only in anticipation

of those Saturdays. I seldom went out, and in an effort to make the time pass more quickly I drowned myself in books and writing. Fortunately, there was still Nicolas, with whom, despite the death of the *Middle Eastern Review*, I continued to dream of future literary fame and fortune. Through our writing would we find immortality. I was still mesmerized by my friend and lived completely in his shadow. Writing was the only area where I felt myself his equal. In fact, I found my ideas more original than his and my style far more brilliant.

And yet today he is the one who has just won the biggest literary prize in the world — short of the Nobel. He's the one basking in glory. As for me, I'm still in his shadow. He writes; I revise and correct. I'm his English publisher. Everyone knows him. No one knows me, except for a few professional colleagues.

At the end of these dark weekly tunnels, these days of melancholy and literature, there was nonetheless a ray of light. Every Saturday I repaired to the funerary chapel to await, with pounding heart, Yasmina's arrival. I always arrived first, to revel in the voluptuous state of anxiety that enveloped me until she appeared, but also to savor the pleasure of seeing her suddenly emerge out of the shadowy light of the crypt.

Then one Saturday she arrived draped in an immaculate tara, which veiled her entire body from head to toe. She looked for all the world like some pagan goddess, a virgin, and she refused to let me touch her. She said she could only stay with me for a few minutes. I looked so utterly distraught that she took pity on me and ran her hands through my hair in a tender gesture.

"Don't forget to come next Saturday," she murmured in my ear.

And then she vanished into the darkness.

I was never to see her again.

On the following two Saturdays I returned to the site of our secret rendezvous. I waited for her there in an indescribable state of worry and despair. And I began to imagine all kinds of terrible things. She had fled back into the desert from which she had come. After all, these bedouin girls were known to be unpredictable and untamable. They preferred the emptiness of the desert sands and winds to the confining life of cities. . . . But that made no sense. I knew that Mansour was an autocrat with his children.

No, I would reassure myself, it's nothing more complicated than that her employers are making her work on Saturdays. Hadn't she told me how demanding they were? Of course, that was it. In the hope of catching a glimpse of her, I would wander for hours throughout the wealthy parts of the city where the Europeans lived. But she was nowhere. . . .

Then it came to me in a flash: she was having an affair with someone else! Of course, that was it! And I was overcome with uncontrollable rage.

After that I imagined the worst. Was it possible that she had been murdered? Could her father, or her brother, have somehow discovered that she had been dishonored, and killed her to cleanse the family of the opprobrium? These crimes of honor among bedouin tribes was not all that uncommon, and for the most part went unsolved and unpunished. From time to time there would be an article in the local paper about some poor woman, identity unknown, who had been found strangled or with a slit throat. And since the authorities could make no inroads into the bedouin's code of silence, there was little or no effort made to solve the crimes. No one was even very shocked by them, for these constantly moving, usually unregistered, members of the population were a law unto themselves.

I spent my days searching for her. I spent my nights searching for her. I suffered more than I knew any human could suffer. If only I could see her, I kept pleading, if only I could see her one more time!

At dusk I would climb the Hill of Tiles and there, leaning against a door to the tombs, as darkness began to fall, I would wait, hoping against hope, in a state of utter despair, petrified in my unhappiness, my eyes fixed on the tent where I had first laid eyes on Yasmina. Through the heavy black wool sides of the tent I could make out the silhouettes of people moving about, as I could hear the sound of voices and laughter coming from inside. Her laughter. No . . . not hers. Hours went by, and finally I would head home, sick with despair, my heart pounding so loudly that I could scarcely tell the difference between its incessant beat and the pounding surf of the nearby sea.

Then, one morning, I saw her picture in the

newspaper. Beneath her lovely face, which death had not disfigured, was the following caption: "The Unknown of the Canal." She had been found on the banks of the Mahmoudieh Canal, stabbed to death. The article went on to say that the autopsy report had indicated that she was pregnant.

Yasmina dead! No, it couldn't be. . . . Yet there it was. And it was all my fault! I burst into tears and could not stop sobbing. I left the house to seek refuge in the streets and walked aimlessly, still sobbing, from one end of town to the other, bearing all the woes of the world in my broken heart. In losing Yasmina, I had lost everything. I could think of nothing but joining her in death. I wanted to throw myself out of a window. No, drowning would be better. I was a murderer, and deserved to die.

For more than thirty years I firmly believed that Mansour had somehow got wind of our romance and had killed Yasmina to avenge his honor.

Chapter 5

The war in Europe, now over a year old, had been for us but a distant event, of no real consequence. It was moreover a dull war, with both sides lined up across from each other only a few miles apart, blustering more than doing battle. The Maginot line was, we had it on good authority, impregnable, and the French army, buttressed by our own stalwart young men, the largest in the world. So why didn't the Germans, and their funny little führer, give up their grandiose plans of expansion and go home?

And then everything changed, virtually overnight. The Germans, knowing they could never pierce the French fortresses by a frontal assault, made an end run around the Maginot line and in a matter of days overran the Netherlands, Belgium, and then, to our utter dismay, France itself. We saw images in our newspapers of thousands upon thousands of Parisians heading south — in overloaded automobiles, pushing bicycles, on foot — holding children by the hand, bearing in their arms whatever precious possessions they had managed to grab. And there were images too of our soldiers at Dunkerque, being loaded helter-skelter onto ships and boats of every make and vintage, escaping just in time the final thrust of the Germans. Even today the memory of those defeats melds in my mind with my own personal tragedy, with the searing memory of my lost love.

And then the French surrender, the shameful handshake at Montoire that put an end to the conflict and installed a lackey government in Vichy — the same city that would play such an important part in my later life. In Egypt the heavily pro-French population — the Syrians, the Jews, the Lebanese — refused to accept that their glorious image of France had been tarnished. They refused to believe the cold hard fact of the defeat. They preferred to believe that France had been betrayed. Surely a miracle would occur to reverse the past few weeks and restore its glory.

We listened to the radio appeal from London by General de Gaulle, but most of the foreign colony, especially the embassy personnel, took it with a grain of salt, as did the ranking officers of the French Mediterranean fleet. Was it opportunism on their part? Military discipline on the part of the French navy? After all, they argued, the newly appointed leader was Marshal Petain, and for most of the French in Egypt, Petain *was* France.

Most of my information about events on the Continent came from Nicolas, who, like me, was finishing his last year of secondary school. We discussed the now-not-so-distant war each time we got together, and assessed our chances of becoming involved. We argued that we were too young, but in our hearts we knew that in all likelihood the war would catch up with us sooner or later.

Despite the cynicism of so many of his compatriots, Nicolas's father made the decision to respond to General de Gaulle's appeal and join his Free French forces in London. Since he was one of the first to respond, and because of his relatively high station in the French diplomatic corps, he became almost immediately one of de Gaulle's top aides. Nicolas stayed on in Alexandria until the school year was out, then rejoined his father in London. Our farewells were cordial, but subconsciously at least, I still harbored a deep resentment at what he had done to our magazine. I had a feeling, too, that our paths would cross again, for not long after Nicolas's father left Egypt, my father was called back to London to join his old army unit.

Thus I was left completely alone, in the weeks and months following Yasmina's death. Once or twice I ran into Elias and Irene, but they cut me dead. I had no one in the world I could talk to, no one with whom I could share my grief. I didn't even know where my beloved was buried. Or, I wondered, had they even accorded her a decent burial? I would have wanted her to lie in that little chapel where we had loved each other so desperately for all those months. I would have liked to see her, to warm her in my arms, to talk to her. But I didn't even have that consolation. I had no memento of her, no shred or rag to clutch in loving memory to my broken heart.

∗   ∗   ∗

War was moving closer, raging now in the nearby Libyan desert, but all the bombs in the world could fall around me, all the victories and defeats of the Allies come and go, I could not have cared less. Air raid alarms were increasingly common, and my mother would urge me to go down into the shelters at the first signal, but I refused. Nothing mattered to me any longer. I barely listened to the staccato of the now-familiar antiaircraft batteries chattering in the night right outside our window, as I barely reacted to the explosions of bombs landing, whether they were distant or near. The only thing that mattered to me now, and even more to my mother, was to rejoin my father in England. But he had made us promise to stay until I had received my diploma from Victoria College. As soon as I had, we booked passage on the next ship, which turned out to be a battered old troop ship. From the docks it looked barely seaworthy. It was unloading troops and ammunition, and for the return trip priority was being given to the elderly and invalids. Any remaining berths were allotted to the likes of us who were being reunited with our families. Rumors were rampant that the waters between here and home were crawling with both German and Italian submarines; in fact, news had just reached us that the proudest ship in the British navy, the *Royal Ark*, had just been sunk. The only redeeming footnote was the report that the *Royal Ark*'s captain, who had somehow miraculously survived, was picked up swimming with one hand, the other hand proudly holding above the waves his braided cap. Surely such spirit and bravery would end up carrying the day!

Till now I had viewed the war through the tear-stained eyes of my own inconsolable grief. But at our first port of call I suddenly came face-to-face with real suffering.

We took on board wounded whose faces were nothing more than a mass of twisted and swollen flesh; others whose faces you could not even see, since they were swathed in bandages; still others whose entire bodies were wrapped in bandages, looking for all the world like the mummies of my former home. But these mummies were still alive. They were soldiers, most of them still in their uniforms, or rather what remained of their uniforms. One or more of their limbs was missing, and they lay on their stretchers, moaning and calling for help. But the nurses on board were few and far between, and horribly overworked. I wanted to help but felt completely inadequate. All I could do was to talk to them and, more often, listen to their stories, and what they had to tell was the apocalypse. Through them I learned the horrors of war, discovered the terrible tempest of History from which my Alexandrian cocoon had till now protected me. But even worse than the stories they told were their silences, the terror I could see in their eyes as they stared into the darkness of their souls. Suddenly I was ashamed of my tanned face, my intact legs and arms, my grief born of love.

London was a nightmare.

Hitler's Luftwaffe was intent on subduing England

by destroying her cities, and the emphasis was clearly on the crown jewel, the capital. I made my way through a city of burned-out walls and endless piles of rubble, out of which, by some unexplained miracle, the intact towers of Saint Paul and Westminster rose in all their majesty.

I had lived a completely self-centered life. I now swore to live a life of heroism, to put my romantic sorrow behind me, to bury my grief once and for all, and to dedicate myself to the greater good, to the fight against evil. I wanted to join the armed forces, become a soldier — and I realized that I had always wanted that since I was a child. One of my ancestors had fought at Waterloo, and now my father had been posted abroad to lead his regiment into battle, and that was where I too should be, right up on the front lines. A wave of patriotism lifted me up and carried me high above myself.

But reality has a way of bringing you back to earth with a resounding thud. My proud and glorious dreams resulted in my being accepted into the army all right, but not on the front lines. My battlefront was an underground office in London, where I was tied to a chair, so to speak, under the pretense that the armed forces needed my brains and my knowledge of languages. It was with great reluctance therefore that I was assigned to a unit known under the general heading of "Documentation," an innocent term that included a multitude of activities for the secret services: decoding, preparation of false documents, counterfeiting, outfitting chosen personnel with all the equipment and identification they would need to perform their various tasks. All that in the third-level basement of the Dorchester Hotel.

I was assigned to the unit specializing in North Africa and the Middle East. To the gargantuan task of dealing with the Axis was added the complex problem of unraveling, and then combatting, the various clandestine Jewish underground movements — the Irgun first and foremost, which from its base in Egypt was operating a network of sabotage aimed at Palestine. An incredible imbroglio of spies and conspirators. To try and figure out exactly what was going on, you had to adopt a quasi–Middle Eastern frame of mind yourself. It was like a tapestry being woven by several often-contradictory hands, each with its own pattern and agenda, and we had to make sense of this seemingly inextricable mess to our emissaries so they could act accordingly. Our job was to furnish our agents with indispensable covers by making sure the documents we provided would pass as authentic.

Within a surprisingly short time I not only adapted myself to but took pride in these clandestine games of the shadow war, and within a few months I had become so adept that I was commended by my superiors. Inks, papers, official stamps, typewriters, encoding and decoding machines — none of this hush-hush paraphernalia held any secrets for me. My knowledge, plus the virtue of patience and that indescribable element known as flair, enabled me almost instinctively to tell the difference between a valid and a phony document. The team of counterfeiters — mostly recruited from prisons specifically to work with us — considered me a past master of the art. They assured me that after the war I had a bright future among them if I was so inclined.

I worked fifteen, sometimes twenty, hours a day, with all the dedication and devotion that my country's beleaguered position deserved. My fatigue helped me bury deep within me the sad memory of Yasmina. I tried to repress any amorous impulse and put my grief behind me. I had lived a useless life till now and felt a certain exhilaration at knowing I was doing something useful. Day after day I hardened myself against the memory of lost love.

And then one day the war came even closer. The dreaded messenger from the War Department arrived to deliver the awful news: my father had fallen at Monte Cassino. We were told that his was a glorious death, but it was death nonetheless. My mother had lived in the daily fear that Father would not return, but when the expectation became reality, she crumbled. I could see her declining day by day. She had had only two loves in her life, Father and me, and now that he was gone she lavished on me all her love and devotion. Yet at the same time a kind of indifference settled over her. She took refuge in some inner world and seemed not to care about the war or the suffering of others. She rarely if ever left our apartment, became totally self-involved; she spent her days listening for my footsteps in the hallway, announcing my return from work, and she sat with her hand by the phone in the hope of hearing my voice, if only announcing I would be home late. She lived on the edge of the void, her door ajar, and in this endless waiting she had lost her winning smile. Tears had furrowed her face with deep wrinkles that made her look twice her age. If I had been transferred to the front, to the front lines of battle, I think she would either have gone mad or given up the ghost. As it was, if I were gone as much as two days she was in a state of indescribable panic.

Please don't misunderstand. She was neither abusive nor possessive: quite simply, she loved me. But her love was a prison. She asked nothing from me except that I be there, but that requirement weighed on me heavily, despite all my love for her.

Looking back, I see as if in a fog the blurred image of the young man I was then, so focused on my work I could barely think of anything else, coming and going from the underground office where I was perfecting my talents as a counterfeiter and the apartment where my mother's love held me in a viselike grip. I often brought her little gifts — a bouquet of flowers, a box of sweets — as a surprise. And I made up stories, amusing anecdotes I had heard firsthand, or sometimes second, to make her smile, rouse her from her torpor.

Months went by, and the war continued above our heads. All I knew of the war was the thunderous sound of bombs falling and the strident whistle of the air raid sirens. Until one day the war descended into the street.

I had had a long, hard day in the office and was on my way home on the bus rather late at night, my head still filled with false papers and impressive, but equally false, stamps and photographs. I was totally unaware of the outside world until I felt my neighbor — a quite pretty girl, in fact — staring at me.

"Excuse me," she said, "but I'm afraid you're sitting on my skirt."

Taken aback, I jumped to my feet.

"So sorry," I managed to say. "Will you ever forgive me?"

"Of course." She smiled. "Why don't you sit down?"

"Thank you. . . . I'm afraid I'm terribly absent-minded."

"You look more as if you're totally exhausted," she said.

After this banal exchange we struck up a conversation that was perfectly natural and — for anyone who knows how shy I am — quite remarkable. And then all of a sudden the sirens went off, and there was a deafening roar. Instinctively I dived for the floor, dragging the girl with me in a protective gesture. And then I lost consciousness.

When I came to there was the dreadful stench of burning flesh in my nostrils. My clothes were drenched with blood. The blood of the young girl who was lying beside me, her head exploded, horribly unrecognizable.

Filled with terror and despair, I began to sob uncontrollably, sobbing for the girl, for myself, for life itself.

In a strange way that shock was therapeutic; it gave me the courage to see the reality of war for the first time, and the strength to react against the apathy that had begun to turn me into a zombie. I took my courage in my hands and, citing the dangers of her remaining in London, sent my mother away to Scotland to stay with a cousin of hers, a paragon of energy and good cheer. She agreed only on the condition that I write her every day.

I then made an effort to go out after work, to live or at least make the effort. Night after night I would force myself to go to a pub, drinking along with the best of them, in the vain hope I might find a willing girl. When that failed, I repaired to bars that catered to soldiers, where there were sure to be girls. But these encounters were disastrous, a complete humiliation — miserable, ridiculous efforts to forget Yasmina. . . .

The first time I took a girl home I blamed the sorry results on abstinence. After all, only once you start eating do you realize how hungry you are, and I hadn't made love since my summer with Yasmina. I blamed the second fiasco on the fact that my partner's oversize buttocks had turned me off. Then I began to wonder seriously: was it possible that at age twenty I was impotent? That Yasmina's death had stripped me forever of my virility? Was it possible that I could never manage to desire, to possess, another woman? Was I bewitched?

At that point I panicked and decided that I had to find some means, however low or sordid, to prove that I could overcome my temporary impotence.

So it was that one night I went to the Wellington, a club that catered to aviators, in search of the Dulcinea who would be the answer to my dreams, when I saw Nicolas again. He appeared to me as if enveloped in a cloud of light, a sort of halo that doubtless existed only in my mind, still deformed as it was with admiration. He was a cross between Gary Cooper and Ernest Hemingway. Film hero, war hero as well. He was born to wear a uniform. His jacket, tightly buttoned, accentuated his broad, athletic shoulders. And all of a sudden I felt like a nobody in my lieutenant's uniform, which till then I had thought made me look quite handsome.

To make things worse, Nicolas was wearing a white silk scarf, draped nonchalantly over his shoulder. No question, life had dealt him a great hand, and the woman he was with, a Ginger Rogers lookalike sculpted in amber, was more than great. Nicolas was staring at her as if she were the only creature on earth.

Why did I feel like running away? Out of shyness? Because I suddenly felt myself very small and insignificant? But it was too late. Nicolas had seen me.

"Edward! Edward!" he called across the crowded room as I was halfway out the door.

"This calls for a bottle of champagne!" he said, after embracing me warmly and introducing me to his companion. And he raised his hand imperiously and ordered a bottle of the best vintage. Then he launched into a harangue, expostulating about "his" war. For him it was the great adventure, a game of Russian roulette. An adventure that could only be played out "up above." What about dying? He could face dying, but not in the mud up to his hips, and not in some back office, some subbasement like the one in which I labored. To die "up there," in the heavens about, a hero's death in the wild blue yonder, now that was the only glorious way to go!

The Ginger Rogers lookalike, who must have heard the same speech a hundred times, wandered away to swivel her hips in front of someone else, leaving Nicolas free to fill me in at length on his endless amorous exploits. . . . My God, I probably couldn't even picture the way the adorable creatures came rushing out to greet his plane as soon as he landed and climbed down out of his cockpit upon returning from some dangerous mission. They couldn't wait to fall into his arms. This living dangerously, these daily brushes with death, seemed to go straight to his balls, he added. He needed to make love in order to calm his nerves, and also because making love was, after all, a hymn to life, now wasn't it, Edward? A hymn you'd better sing as often as you could because, God knows, the next mission might be your last. So he took every available opportunity that came his way: nurses, women from the auxiliary corps, women whose husbands were away at the front, widows . . . you name it. "Quite a collection if I do say so myself. Like the glutton who can't get enough no matter how much he has eaten. I amaze even myself."

He didn't even bother to ask about my father, not to mention my mother. Nor did he seem the least interested in what I might be doing to help the war effort.

Every man for himself was his motto, and the only man he was interested in, the only man he had time for, was himself. He was purely and simply blind to anyone else. I felt he would be nothing but a negative force in my life and made up my mind not to see him again.

And yet only a few brief weeks later I did see him again, this time at Queen Victoria Hospital. His plane had been badly shot up in the course of a mission over Germany, and he had just managed to nurse it back across the channel, making a crash landing from which he had barely escaped alive. He had been in a coma for three days. Even now, after having regained consciousness, his temperature hovered between 104 and 105 degrees, despite the ice-filled blankets he was bundled in. In the beds around him I found once again the same sad collection of human misery I had encountered on the old troop ship that had brought me back to England: men whose bodies had been burnt beyond recognition, others with an arm or leg missing — sometimes both — still others whose faces had been blown to smithereens.

My position as an officer in His Majesty's Special Services opened more than a few doors to me, including those of the military hospitals. Thus I had the opportunity to question the doctors and nurses about Nicolas's medical situation and its possible evolution. They told me that he was suffering from multiple traumas, and said that they were at this point unwilling to make any medical pronouncements about the possible consequences of the accident. On this, my first visit since hearing the news of the crash in the newspapers, Nicolas was bandaged from head to toe. Heavily sedated, he gazed at me from his bed with glazed eyes, and I could tell that he hadn't the faintest notion who I was.

I returned to the hospital every night I was not on duty, and he seemed to enjoy my visits. His dangerously high temperature had been brought under control, and he seemed to be gaining strength each time I saw him. He vaguely remembered an explosion in the fuselage of his plane, then nothing else. In the bed next to him a dying patient was moaning lugubriously, and a few beds farther on another badly wounded soldier was raving deliriously in his sleep. Each day a new cargo of devastated bodies and damaged minds arrived in the old hospital, at such a rate that the doctors and nurses were overwhelmed. The operating rooms were busy around the clock, and some surgeons were working as much as twenty hours a day. The rooms were overcrowded, and beds had to be set up in the hallways to accomodate new arrivals, some of whom remained for days on end on the stretchers on which they had been brought in. The smell of disinfectants permeated the corridors. Several days later, profiting from the fact that he was on special treatment, Nicolas was put into a private room, sheltered from the odors and screams of the wards. That privacy seemed to be more therapeutic than any miracle medicine might have been. His migraines abated, and his speech, which had been badly slurred, rapidly became normal.

Nicolas's stay in the hospital was a boon to our relations. No jealousy, no perversity, shadowed my feelings toward him. I even enjoyed listening to him talk, hearing his memories of war, long monologues that I was careful not to interrupt, sensing that in the endless flow of words he was finding release from all the pent-up nervous tension built up over the past several years when he had daily risked his life. I even found his self-indulgent speeches somehow touching. . . . Nothing serious could befall him, he was convinced. He had a lucky star, and death could not reach him. Death was for the others. He surrounded himself with good-luck charms, amulets and fetishes that he had brought back with him from Egypt, and he never flew a mission without his trusty stuffed koala bear in his cockpit. He also wore a special flying jacket modeled after the suit of light worn by a bullfighter, convinced that if his plane was gored, as he put it, his matador's cape would take the horn, not he. Of course he knew fear, as everyone did, but fear was part of the game. Several times he had returned to his home base with his plane riddled with bullet and shrapnel holes. Several times he had had to make emergency landings, his plane engulfed in flames, and climbed out intact.

He maintained that for him aerial combat was like so many beams of light, so many fiery explosions. He thanked his lucky stars that he had not been a pilot in World War I, when there were real dogfights, when opposing pilots went at it one-on-one, flying so close that they could not only see each other's faces but, as they say, the whites of their eyes.

"I never see the eyes, or even the face, of my opponent — he who is going to die," he said soberly. "At most there is a vague shadow of a person that blends into the cockpit. I have the impression I'm shooting down a machine, not a man."

It was as if he had a protective layer around him that colored both the way he saw things and the choices he made. He recalled the "fun" he had had — that was the word he used — chasing the V-1 rockets the Germans launched against London and described how he used to "take care of them" in midair. For him it was like a sporting event, and he described it in sporting terms.

"Just try and picture it, Edward! First, you put your plane at full throttle, you rev it up to full speed to catch up to the V-1, then you slow down and slip your wingtip ever so gently under the aileron of the bomb, all the while reciting your paternosters, because you never know. . . . But still, that's the easy part. The next stage is the real bone-chiller. What you do now is a quick barrel roll, the point being to try and destabilize the V-1's gyroscope. Some ballet, eh? . . . First you rub up against the bomb, you make solid contact, you bank away and at the same time head the nose straight down in case the damn thing goes off, so that its shock waves won't kill you. And the rest is in the hands of the gods. A man ought to have his head examined, no?"

And at the same time he was relating these hair-raising stories, he could ramble on endlessly about his chief mechanic's fox terrier, a dog that bore the unlikely name of Dollar, who apparently loved Nicolas more than anyone or anything in the world. When he described the way Dollar used to greet him upon his arrival back at the base after a mission, his voice would choke up and there were tears in his eyes. There was at this point in Nicolas's life a curious mixture of complete lack of feeling on the one hand and, on the other, a sensibility that bordered on the maudlin, a characteristic that had perhaps always been present but that the war had brought out even more. And that compassion — if that is what it really was — extended to all the creatures on the face of the earth and in the waters below, from moths to whales, from crows to crocodiles.

However mad and oblivious he may have been, the fact remains that by the end of the war he had racked up ten proven victories in the air, ten enemy aircraft shot down. That made him an ace, and a recognized war hero, and I could only admire this Icarian side of him. His was a glory I could only dream about.

One day, after he had revealed virtually all of his exploits and future plans to me, he admitted that he had started writing a novel about his war experiences. So he had not merely been living a wartime life of follies and festivities, he had also been thinking about what it all meant. "And I mean thinking long and hard," he added. "No matter how tired or cold I was," he said, "I always took the time to write down my thoughts and impressions."

At times his memory seemed to fail him, and he became confused about the chronology of events, remembering only bits and pieces. I was especially struck by this when he told me the story of his final mission.

"I remember very clearly shepherding this crippled B-17 back home," he said. "The plane had taken a lot of German flak over Bremen, and looked like a wreck. There were bullet and shrapnel holes from the antiaircraft batteries from one end of the plane to the other. The plane's machine-gun stations were simply gone, wiped out. One of its motors was on fire, spouting black smoke, which made it virtually impossible for the pilot to see. Both the copilot and navigator had been killed, and the pilot himself wounded. In fact, the cockpit itself had been virtually demolished by a direct hit, and I couldn't help wondering how anyone in there had survived. Anyway, I had to adjust my speed downward to keep pace with this ghost-plane, which sometimes I could barely see because of the dark trail of smoke pouring out of its various wounds. I had picked up the plane over the North Sea, so we had a hell of a ways to go to make it home. And our slow speed made us a perfect target for both enemy anti-aircraft and any planes that might pick up our trail. All I could do was grit my teeth and play the good shepherd, knowing that at any moment the damn thing might explode in my face, taking me with it. But, by God, we did make it back: I remember vividly how I felt when I saw the white cliffs of Dover looming in the distance. And I knew that a few minutes later we'd reach the edge of the highway that had been designated for emergency landings in just such cases."

"So then what happened? How did the B-17 manage to set down?"

"I beg your pardon?" Nicolas said, his eyes suddenly glazed.

"I said, how did the mission end? How did it finally turn out?"

"How did what turn out?"

"But the story you've been telling me, Nicolas."

"I'm sorry, but I don't know what you're talking about. I need to get some rest."

I was completely taken aback. Although he seemed to have recovered so fully from his accident, I realized that he was still suffering from some sort of memory loss. At the time I attributed it to the trauma he had suffered. One does not recover all that quickly from a plane crash that serious. But as time went on I had to face up to the harsh facts. Nicolas was indeed suffering from partial amnesia. Or, more accurately, there were repeated gaps in his memory, especially covering the several-week period prior to his accident. Apparently it wasn't terribly serious. I thought that in time he would recover his full memory, as was generally the case of those who had suffered regressive amnesia.

Taking advantage of my position as a member of the prestigious Dorchester group, I asked the head nurse — who greatly appreciated the concern I had shown for her patient — if I could have a look at Nicolas's medical records. She was reluctant at first, but assured that as his closest friend my request was legitimate, she finally produced his file, reminding me as she handed it over that this should remain completely confidential. Despite all the medical jargon I had to plow through, I was able to ascertain that one of the specialists at Queen Victoria Hospital had picked up and duly noted the problem, which he considered serious. He had not only carefully noted all the disturbing symptoms, he had also stressed that, in his professional view, they could be recurring, and voiced his opinion that Nicolas should not fly again. The other medical reports were more or less routine and made no mention of the recurrent amnesia problem, but focused on the rapid physical recovery he had made in general. I closed the file with a feeling of sadness, but at the same time, I have to confess, a tinge of satisfaction. If I had understood the report correctly, Nicolas's flying days were over. The hero of the wild blue yonder had been grounded. Never again would he take the controls of a Spitfire.

On a sudden impulse, I reopened the medical file, removed the specialist's damning report, and slipped it into my pocket. Nicolas already had enough problems to cope with in this hospital. If he were to learn the contents of the specialist's report, there was no telling what it might do to him.

A fortnight later, immediately after he was released from the hospital, General de Gaulle himself pinned on Nicolas's breast the medal of honor for "extreme bravery and heroic conduct in battle."

Why did I keep that medical report, which indicated not only that Nicolas had amnesia but that it might someday surface again? I swear by all that's holy that at the time I did it solely out of pity, to spare him any possible pain. But perhaps, subconsciously, was it also to serve my own purposes, whatever they might be, if I needed a weapon against Nicolas in the future?

Today this document is carefully filed away in my desk drawer, together with other mementos of my past life. It sits there patiently, awaiting its appointed hour.

Chapter 6

The plane was due to arrive at London's Heathrow Airport at three-thirty. It doubtless would have been on time had it not been for the usual imponderable, in the instance a sudden and violent storm that materialized out of nowhere and forced us to circle the airport interminably. The wind screamed, and our plane was tossed about like a fly in the pipe of a church organ.

I felt uncomfortable at first, then was overcome with panic. The plane was going to crash, I was sure. And unlike Nicolas, there was no way I would ever walk away from it.

Wasn't that the story of our respective lives? He'd been born with a silver spoon in his mouth, whereas my life had been jinxed. If Nicolas had died in that crash, he would have died a hero's death, gone down in a blaze of glory. Posthumous medals would have been bestowed upon him, endless speeches made in his honor. Me? At most a couple of lines in a newspaper article: "A British Airways plane on its way from Paris to Heathrow crashed in the English Channel yesterday afternoon, apparently a victim of the violent storm that struck the area without warning. All four crew members and the thirty-six passengers on board are presumed dead. Among them is the well-known English publisher, Sir Edward Destry. . . ."

Leaving nothing behind, I might add. No widow, no descendants, no literary work. Nothing. What is the death of a sterile man, after all? Like the death of a withered fig tree. Good riddance. The only person who will shed a tear or two will be my secretary. Maybe my godson Peter, too. Peter still needed me; I had seen to that as well.

The captain came onto the loudspeaker and urged us to remain calm. Keep your seat belts securely fastened. We had to be patient, ride out the storm. We had plenty of fuel, enough for us to keep circling for over an hour, he assured. Now and then through a break in the clouds, we could see the airport lights below. The delay gave me plenty of time to go over my plans for revenge. I needed to feed my feelings of resentment, more than ever now, for in the next few hours I was going to drop the bomb that would wipe out my esteemed friend and colleague, Nicolas Fabry. Just a few more hours and I would be redeemed.

That is, if the heavens were willing!

For me the war and early postwar blend into a kind of single, grayish, slightly ill-defined sketch. In 1945 I exchanged my windowless horizon for a view on a university courtyard, my underground desk at the

Dorchester for a seat in the poorly heated amphitheater of a dilapidated university, where the survivors of an earlier war dispensed their presumed wisdom with a boredom that permeated the entire institution.

With my master's degree in hand, I went forth into the big world, ready to make my mark. I was convinced that I had not shown my true mettle during the war, but now I would. Now I would distinguish myself in the world of literary creation. In no time at all my genius as a writer would be remarked and appreciated. My brain was ablaze with noble subjects to write about, my mind crammed with a welter of dark and mysterious plots and scintillating dialogues. Poems, fully rhymed, came to me as easily as bright water flowing over cool mountain stones. I was in turn a poet, a novelist, a playwright, an essayist. And in each guise I was fully aware of my enormous talent. The only problem was, when I put these roiling fantasies to paper and published them in the university literary reviews, their mediocrity became glaringly apparent. My style ranged from the artificial to the forced. It was as flat and redundant as the Yorkshire moors and just as empty.

My beautiful revolts, my grand rebellion, soon became little more than the convulsive movements of a fish out of water. . . . Then, crucified by the evidence, I realized what the problem was. Yes, it was I and I alone who had sentenced myself to mediocrity, to punish myself for the death of Yasmina. I had in a way created my own fate, and as long as this fate held me prisoner, I might indeed have perfect pitch in the abstract, but when it came to the real world I sang out of tune.

Having come to that conclusion, seeing clearly for the first time, I abandoned my literary ambitions and made up my mind to go into publishing. You cast your net and hope it comes up with a decent fish. Mine did, in that I had the good fortune to meet an elderly publisher, blessed with brains and erudition, an eccentric man looking for a colleague with a good head on his shoulders and an excellent critical sense. I grabbed the opportunity and went to work for Turner Press with an enthusiasm and dedication that soon earned me the paternal affection — and, I may say, admiration — of Archibald Turner.

If the poor man had had any idea to what use I would later put the knowledge I was storing up, especially that gleaned from the training course he obliged me to take at a local printing plant, he would have been horrified. Me too, for that matter.

It was not long before I became completely caught up in my new profession, though I confess that as I was reading the manuscripts of others, and seeing their books through to publication, I had to suppress a jealousy that would overcome me now and then. I was the nursemaid, raising other people's children. I guided them, I corrected them, I helped improve them. It was my way of repressing the throbbing pain I felt on many occasions that the works published did not bear my signature, no matter how much I had contributed to their success editorially.

Mother had returned home to London immediately after the war, and I was delighted to see her. My wartime forays into the big world, into London nightlife, came to an end, and once again I would return home most evenings to take care of Mother. I could see that she was declining. I was terrified to see that, day by day, life was draining from her, and I was afraid to leave her alone. What was more, she had a sixth sense that seemed to alert her each time my work was due to keep me away from London, and she would suffer immediate, frightening attacks of panic.

As a result I spent as many evenings as possible at home, in a kind of affectionate inertia. I would hold my mother's hand for hours on end, telling her everything I had done during the day. I doubtless should have been bored to death by my own passivity, and had I been I would surely have reacted. But I did not. To react takes energy, and I had none. I did not rebel against that reclusive existence; I was devoid of desire, stripped completely of the quality of impatience.

The arrival of spring, of warm days and budding trees, should have roused me from my lethargy, but it did not. My blood was cold. There was no blinding light, no singular pleasure, no mad desire that invaded my being. I surveyed myself calmly, living at the edge of myself, as if I were afraid of finding my true self, of finding out what I really wanted. I sometimes had the impression that I had a Siamese twin living inside me and that I was waiting to hear from him, to find out what he wanted me to do. Actually, I haven't the faintest notion what I was waiting for, since I did nothing to make it happen. Which, in fact, is what most people do.

As for my sex life, it was a vast desert. The radiant image of Yasmina, the memory of her caresses, held me prisoner. Other women struck me as hideous and obscene. I found the entire female sex repugnant. In all fairness, I have to say that it was not as though I was fighting off droves of adoring ladies. I was the type whom only his secretary finds appealing. My secretary, the aforementioned Doris, was perfect: diligent, devoted, efficient, and unattractive, which made me feel comfortable with her. Her unprepossessing, rather horsey face had a gentleness that I found touching. There was not the barest hint of emotional entanglement between us; at least, so I had thought until that night when we had both remained in the office to finish up an especially urgent manuscript. In a moment of affection, and to thank her for staying late and helping me, I embraced her as we were saying good night. She misunderstood my hug and held me close, turned her face toward mine, her lips slightly opened in anticipation of the kiss that would surely follow. But instead of Doris's face beneath me I saw that of my beloved Yasmina, and I was filled with a feeling of revulsion. I pushed her roughly away, and poor Doris burst into tears. I hate tears and will go to almost any lengths to avoid them. I tried to make amends, apologizing for my reaction, which, I assured her, had nothing to do with her. Then I decided to open my heart to her, and told her the story of my long-lost love, my Yasmina, who had made it impossible for me ever to love another woman. Did she believe me? I am not sure, but the fact is Doris has remained devoted to me to this day.

That same evening, by a strange twist of fate, I took home with me a Greek midshipman whose ship happened to be in port, a young chap I had picked up in a Soho pub. Even as I write these lines, I am amazed that I can do so with such detachment. Nor is my memory playing tricks on me. I was not drunk, and each minute of that night will remain forever engraved in my body as well as my mind.

I am not making any excuses for my conduct, nor do I think I need to. Whenever I look into the mirror of my conscience, I feel not the slightest twinge of shame. After all, does it really matter whether one goes with a man or a woman? To make love without love always ends with a similar feeling of dissatisfaction and, indeed, disgust when it's over. I had to do something to exorcise the ghost of Yasmina from my life. In my memory of the evening the Greek sailor was a genderless creature, a partner, a simple prolongation of my solitary fantasies. But whenever I think of Nicolas, I cannot help comparing the exhilarating tumult of his sex life with the absurdity of my own. And whenever I think back to Nicolas's own past, I remember with unbridled hatred the enormous crime, the dire act, for which he bears full responsibility.

During the time I was picking up one Greek sailor after another and publishing other people's manuscripts, Nicolas was crisscrossing the world, writing up a storm and breaking hearts.

His parents had been killed in an automobile accident in 1945, leaving him well off. After leaving the service, Nicolas had taken the competitive examinations for entrance into the school for future diplomats and passed them brilliantly. Perhaps he had chosen that path in memory of or in deference to his father; more likely it was his thirst for adventure and travel that had motivated him. I like to think that if he emerged from his studies near the top of the class it was because the Foreign Office, rebuilding its image and staff after the war, was looking to recruit those whose wartime activities were beyond reproach. The jury whose job it was to evaluate the graduating class was, I am told, especially lenient toward this war hero because of his "exceptional services in the cause of Liberation." Personally, I refuse to believe that the high marks he received were based on merit alone.

His first diplomatic post disappointed him greatly. Hoping for high adventure, he landed in a country whose landscape was as flat as its challenges: Belgium. Nonetheless, instead of yielding to boredom and the Wallony mists he put the time to good use by writing his wartime memoirs, reconstituting in exquisite detail the fog-shrouded atmosphere of the British airfields. Like so many veterans, he felt the overriding need to recount the war as he had lived it. Whenever he got bogged down in the writing, he fled to Paris in search of the ideal publisher for his work, which he had tentatively entitled *Cross-Channel Memoirs*. For the most part he was getting a rather chilly reception. The last thing the French wanted to read about in those early postwar days were stories about exemplary deaths.

But Nicolas was not a man to give up easily.

Whether the public liked it or not — or rather, despite what the publishers thought — he intended to write about those young men who had given their lives for freedom.

One day the phone rang, and my secretary said that Mr. Fabry was on the line.

"Edward," he said, and I could tell he was calling to announce good news — that is, good news for himself. "I've found a publisher for my first book. He tells me he loves the manuscript, but I know better. He's a cagey old fellow, but I can see right through him. He doesn't like my subject any better than the other publishers I've submitted it to, and he knows the marketplace isn't ready for it. But what he sees is a bright new title, a new name to add to his stable."

So there it was! Nicolas was going to be a published author. And from his words — "I've found a publisher for my *first* book" — it was evident that he planned to write others.

And indeed he did. His second book, *The Great Ball*, was a fiasco. Which didn't deter Nicolas, who went on to write a third; *Guanamoroso*, which was published a year later, won one of the more prestigious literary prizes that year, and earned him the jealousy of his fellow diplomats. Nicolas was on his way. A small name, but a name nonetheless. His passage from anonymity to relative fame struck him as perfectly normal, for he was convinced that he was a genius. When I think that Balzac complained of his mediocrity, that he kept telling everyone that he lacked talent and the inspiration to go with it! But self-doubt was a quality Nicolas lacked.

It goes without saying that I became Nicolas's English publisher. Not only that, but the translator of his masterpieces. I could have left well enough alone and simply translated them, but no, I had to do more, much more than that, I had to fiddle with them, improve on them, for in some curious way I considered myself the real author of these works. I was convinced that by some strange magic Nicolas had tapped into my soul and turned to his advantage the rich vein of creativity buried within me. I discovered in his works harmonics that were mine and mine alone, though stifled and suppressed, deformed and denatured by his mediocre interpretation. I was the composer, Nicolas nothing more than the interpreter of my music, and a clumsy one at that. So as I had done so many years before in Alexandria, reworking and rewriting his abominable short story, I took his raw manuscript and made it better. I blue-penciled his endless redundancies, I gave his vague ideas substance, I replaced his clichés and platitudes with phrases that had bite and flavor. I took his skeletons and gave them flesh, for his plots of passionate love and high adventure, with inevitably exotic backgrounds, were as thin as ice in September. All the characters were distressingly alike, papier-mâché creatures devoid of flesh and blood; and at the center of every plot was the all-conquering Don Juan himself.

Never in any of the novels was there a sense of commitment, an effort to deal with a serious problem. As in his novels, so in his life. A smattering of ideas and desires waiting to be fulfilled in his life, to be rendered cogent in his writing. To him tragedy was anathema. Misfortune and suffering turned him off immediately. He operated on helium — anything lighter than air — and when he couldn't figure where to go next in his tale, he'd head for the heavens. He merely sketched in his characters, filled in his settings in broad strokes. My role was to come behind, fill in the blanks, turn the sketch into a finished painting.

An unfulfilling role? Perhaps, but I have to say I took a certain albeit dubious pleasure in playing that part. The world may not have known, but I knew that Nicolas's success in Great Britain, and indeed in the English-speaking world, was my work. Nicolas owed me that glory. And because the novels were not signed by me, because they bore the name of Nicolas Fabry, all my creative inhibitions disappeared, and I felt free to exercise my "talents" to the fullest.

Never once did Nicolas mention the work I put in on his novels, never once did he even allude to the changes. He seemed completely unaware of these "translations."

He was handsome, wealthy, and elegant. He was a diplomat. And with literary fame added to the mix, Nicolas was fast becoming a celebrity. From his post in Belgium he had been transferred to Ankara, where word of his fame and good looks had preceded him, so that he was in constant demand at every embassy in the city. Women fought for the privilege of being seen in his company, yielding to his seductive charms without exception: those of previously impeccable virtue as much as those known to be coquettes, princesses as much as commoners. He mistreated them? They kissed his hand. He threw them over? They came crawling back.

He explained his conduct by saying that he needed "to spend his life between his ladies' legs" to keep his equilibrium, to maintain his mental center of gravity. He went on to say that he did his best to concentrate his affairs of the heart on chance encounters. Simple Is Best was his motto. He especially enjoyed natural, spontaneous liaisons. And here in Ankara, his preference ran to non-French-speaking partners, where the lack of a common language filtered out everything but the essential, so that only what he called "an exchange of elementary feelings" seeped through. He took as his own Victor Hugo's pregnant sentences: "I look upon women as Vauban looking upon fortresses. They are there to be taken. The only question is how much time you should spend on each."

"There's not a grain of ethnology in my makeup," Nicolas used to say, "but there dwells within me an insatiable curiosity about all forms of life, about every sensibility. I do not believe that my endless quest for the various wellsprings of human nature can be equated with Don Juanism. It's a veritable passion, almost vampirism. And in these prophylactic liaisons — sorry for the pun, old boy! — I am constantly discovering treasures that by their tenderness, the confidence they engender, the generosity they reveal, are simply shattering. What I can offer in return is pitiable in comparison."

Having opted to live in the temporary, to savor the provisional, Nicolas had learned to love only the present moment, not just the day but the hour, the very minute, of pleasure enjoyed. For him it was infinite happiness. Therein perhaps lay the true reason for his apparently insatiable need to conquer.

He went on plucking women the way most people pluck grapes from a vine, until the day he fell in love, however incredible that may seem. He was then in Canada, where he was first secretary at the French embassy, and from all reports he loved everything about the country: the vast stretches of open, still unsettled country; the searing heat of summer; the bone-chilling cold of winter; the "hilarious accent," as Nicolas described it, of the French Canadians. He wrote me lyrical, wildly enthusiastic letters about the place. He was, in short, a happy man.

When Anne came into his life — at approximately page six of his Canadian adventure, the way heroines of pulp-fiction novels appear — he suddenly realized for the first time "how empty and sterile his life up till then had been." To quote one of his letters: "My earlier life, my dear Edward, has been nothing but one long yawn." He had never known what it was to feel this way, and he plunged headlong, but with eyes presumably open, into the sublime adventure commonly known as monogamy.

Anne Delariviere had been sent to the French embassy to get some information about pursuing her studies in France. She was studying psychology, and after receiving her undergraduate degree in Canada had been awarded a fellowship to obtain the equivalent of a master's degree in France. The orderly on duty had sent her to see the cultural attaché, and as chance would have it his door was closed, so she took the liberty of going to the office next door, which happened to be Nicolas's.

At first sight — to coin a phrase — Nicolas fell, hook, line, and sinker. For the first time he glimpsed the pit of passion into which he had so often managed to avoid falling. Anne fell just as hard, as had all her many predecessors.... Three months later she was pregnant. It was at this period that I met her for the first time, during one of their lightning visits to London, and I too immediately fell under her spell.

To say she was beautiful was an understatement. Her long, flowing blond tresses framed a finely sculpted, alabaster face in which were set two enormous sapphire eyes. So white was her skin, in fact, that one could follow every inch of the delicate maze of her veins. When she smiled, it was as if the sun had just shone through a bank of clouds. Her legs were long and lithe, and the firm roundness of her bust was irresistible; no matter how one tried, one's eyes would inevitably be drawn to it.

The woman was luminous — no other word will do — she shone like one of those opaline lamps that used to grace my grandmother's Victorian living room.

I couldn't refrain from thinking that never would such a sublime creature as this fall in love with me. Never. Me the graceless, charmless, talentless one, the Mr. Nobody who, with my thirtieth year staring me in the face, was beginning to go bald! Me, Mr. Boring himself, the obscure pen-pusher whose task in this world was to correct the spelling and syntax of others. No, there would be no Anne Delariviere in my life. I had had my brief moment of happiness with Yasmina. Now it was over. My opportunity was dead and gone. Murdered. Cast out. Buried. And I was jealous of Nicolas as I watched him gaze lovingly and in wonder at his wife's belly, as if he could see through her, as if the shape of their future child was visible to him.

The birth a few weeks later of their son, Pierre-Yves-Dominique, later to be known as Peter, was, according to Nicolas, "the most important moment of his life." I became the child's godfather, and I went to Montreal for the christening. My mother had died only a short while before, leaving me distressed and forlorn, thinking of all the things I could have done as a son to better her lot, but also leaving me free at long last of her confining presence.

Anne struck me as changed. Radically changed. She was pale, her former glowing health dimmed. She looked dull, almost tarnished, far from the radiant, blossoming new mother. It took me only two days to figure out why: Nicolas was stifling her by slow degrees. When you got right down to it, for Nicolas this superb beauty was no more than a mound of clay that he was intent on shaping as he saw fit, to squeeze into the mold of his own whims and caprices. Anne Delariviere should above all be Mrs. Fabry, the meek servant of a despotic master.

In taking care of her, Nicolas was taking care of himself, his comfort, his image. He wanted people to admire her so that they would in effect be admiring him. He wanted her to be cultured, so that her savoir-faire would redound to his advantage.

He dressed her in accordance with his own tastes,

according to his own image, the only image he had ever truly loved. And before long she lost that wonderful smile as she began to let herself go, turned her back on her own personality, abdicated to her husband's desires.

"He doesn't let me breathe," she confided to me one day.

And yet, even as he continued to proclaim to the rooftops how madly in love with her he was, to play with words, he was at the same time playing the fool to try and conceal the true emptiness of that love, that public display of mad passion. Before long Nicolas began to stay away for long stretches, and when he was in town he would often come home late in the evening. He was adept at inventing sudden rendezvous — some in far-off places. In short, barely six months after the birth of their son, Nicolas was back at his old habits, reverting to the insatiable satyr he doubtless was at heart. When Anne began to make scenes, he made fun of her, called her stubborn, possessive, and infantile, argued that she left no room for sharing, whereas he, despite his love for her, was undemanding. Love, he explained, did not imply exclusivity.

When it became clear that Nicolas intended to live by his words, Anne informed him that she had no intention of joining him after he had been appointed to a diplomatic post in Africa. Nicolas informed her that she could do as she liked, but she should know that he intended to take Peter with him. Anne filed for divorce.

My role in their separation was not negligible. During the early days I remained on the sidelines, very much the spectator, watching first one then the other, listening to the secrets they each confided in me, rejoicing inwardly at the rapid disintegration of their marriage — which represented Nicolas's failure. A perverse sense of duty nonetheless made me try to warn him.

"Nicolas, you're playing with fire here. You can't treat Anne that way and not expect it to backfire."

His response was as swift as it was scathing: "What do you know about women, Edward?"

I did not respond, but I showed him in my own sweet way that my knowledge of feminine psychology was not exactly nil. My first revenge on Nicolas was to work ever so subtly on Anne, not by encouraging her to stick with him or give him another chance but by helping her free herself from his clutches entirely. Without her knowing it, I became her confidant and mentor.

Using words filled with friendship and tenderness for my old friend Nicolas, I slipped in just the right clever, perfidious poison. Pretending to praise him, I all but buried him. One has no idea, really, how easy it is to suggest ill of someone under the thinnest guise of barbed compliments. I made Anne understand that her husband was a man without depth, a man with a mask to the world, an errant playboy, a charlatan. A phony. And I took enormous pleasure in seeing her love begin to crack and break up, like the icebound Saint Lawrence River in the thawing spring.

Nicolas was the first to be surprised by this new turn of events as he saw his wife's feelings toward him change, veer away, disappear. I sincerely believe he was not only taken aback but hurt. For once. Perhaps for the first and only time in his life. Thus his departure for Central Africa took on the appearance of flight, as if he were running away from a situation that he couldn't control. He talked of resigning from the diplomatic corps. "Embassy life is so sterile, you know," he would say, "and so demanding." So it was not as if his thoughts of quitting were an effort to win back his wife and son — who it turned out he did not finally take with him to his new post — but simply because there was nothing more to be gained from the "career." It was intruding on his other life, his "work" — his writing — which was taking more and more of his time.

His next three novels — *Flight of Eagles, The Mountebanks,* and *Wild Oats* — were all solid successes, but with each new work his imagination seemed to freeze up a trifle more. Traveling, in the past a source of inspiration, no longer seemed to work. Actually, if he had accepted that far-flung post in Central Africa, it had been for the sole purpose of trying to get his flagging creative juices flowing again. To no avail: the steaming tropics seemed, if I may be permitted the expression, to leave him cold. He wrote me long, despairing letters, which I must say did move me.

What a void this place is! No Anne. No Peter. I miss Peter enormously. But what in the world would a four-year-old child do here under this blistering, unrelenting sun? I would love to drown myself in my work but here that is quite out of the question. Everything is geared to making sure we remain as idle as possible. My peers and superiors seem bound and intent on making sure we get bogged down in a world of

91

exasperating calm. I try to fight my boredom by gal-
loping full tilt on horseback through the brush and by
flying a local plane, to keep my hand in.

Or again this letter, written a few weeks later, from
Nicolas-the-Exhibitionist, still intent on making sure
one didn't forget what a heartthrob he was.

As for my love life, zero. Think of me in that context as
an anorexic. I'm working on my divorce as slowly as
possible. I don't want you to think from the above that
I've turned celibate, for in fact I do have my fair share
of European women here — mostly hysterical, generally more concerned about keeping thin than anything
else — and if I do yield now and again to their presumed charms it is without conviction, to keep my
hand in (so to speak; sorry, Edward, you'll edit that),
and to uphold the honor of France here in the colonies.
In this remote city my every movement is followed
and commented on. I remember with great fondness
my years in Belgium. That was provincial too, God
knows, but there at least I was free to come and go at
will. Here I'm stifled, choking to death. To boot, no
chance of tasting the exotic delicacies that abound here.
Verboten. The local beauties, it has been made emi-
nently clear to me, are strictly off-limits. Edward, you
should see their breasts — most of the time they go
about uncovered — golden and sculpted by the gods.
In short, I'm bored to death.

To make things worse, the political side of my job is
completely frustrating.

As a former colonial power, France has what I
would term a despot complex — especially in the light
of the Algerian war — and we have to back and protect
any local tinpot dictator who comes to power in
Africa, which means having to either ignore or approve

of the cruelty and torture that seems part of their baggage. So here I am supporting these monsters, and their policy of exterminating this tribe or that — everything is so tribal here, Edward — all in the name of democracy, of peoples' right to dispose of their own future. The whole thing makes me sick.

Despite the dismal tone of his letters, that postcolonial experience ended up producing a novel, entitled *Chevara Go,* which was rather fierce, even cruel, but very successful. So successful, in fact, that it gave Nicolas the courage to resign from the diplomatic service. I still have the letter, written after he had been in Africa for two years, in which he announced the news.

Farewell Africa! Good-bye diplomatic service! It's been a long time since I felt so good about something I did. I just handed in my resignation, and I have no intention of going back on my decision, despite the pressures I've been getting from the Foreign Office in Paris strongly suggesting I take an extended holiday — on sick pay, to recover from overwork! As if one could overwork here in Central Africa even if one wanted to! My intransigence is nourished by my irremediable disgust for the diplomatic service. Nor am I motivated by anything sentimental, or by lowly politics. It's rather because of that unsullied image of France that I had during the war, the France I fought for so long and hard. And to think that you are forever berating me, my dear Edward, for lacking in idealism! For years I've suffered — physically suffered — from the drama of our lost empire. That beautiful dream of my youth. That is doubtless why I prefer to turn my back on this daily comedy that I am forced to play in my fancy ambassador's uniform. Good-bye hypocrisy. I am leaving my talented colleagues and diplomatic brethren the task of explaining to the world just how the influence and importance of France, and French culture, is growing in direct proportion to the loss of her overseas possessions. . . .

How in the world was I ever to believe in his profession of patriotic faith when I knew there was only one single thing whose influence and importance he was interested in — the career of one Nicolas Fabry? No, it was not some deep-seated concern about France that made him quit the world of diplomacy, not some high-minded set of principles; it was his concern about his literary career. Period.

So Nicolas returned to Paris without a worry in the world. Free as air. He didn't have to worry about money, for in addition to what his parents had left him he was receiving a generous monthly draw from his French publisher irrespective of the sales of his books, and the income from his foreign sales was by now becoming meaningful. In the English-speaking countries, the United Kingdom and the United States especially, his sales figures were beginning to exceed our wildest expectations — in good part thanks to my promotional efforts. Not to mention the extensive rewriting and editing I did. Yes, it was thanks to me that Nicolas's novels had become best-sellers.

Chapter 7

While Nicolas was busy making a name for himself as a writer, I too had become a publishing success. With the small inheritance left to me by my mother, I bought back the Turner Press — to the enormous delight of an elderly Archibald, who more and more regarded me as his adopted son. I immediately increased the number of books the press published. One success bred another, and our list grew until soon I had to employ battalions of new editors, assistants, and secretaries to help with the volume of business. These were heady times. We moved into an elegant building off Regent Street. I opened an American affiliate. In addition to an enviable stable of prestigious house authors such as Vladimir Nabokov, Samuel Beckett, Lawrence Durrell, and Romain Gary, Turner Press boasted the most promising young talent from around the world. I, Edward Destry, had become one of the most influential publishers in the world — renowned, respected, and in due course knighted.

The pace of my life was madness itself. I routinely worked fifteen-hour days and through the weekend, unable to slow down, like a bicyclist afraid that if he stops pedaling he will fall.

A few minor commercial disasters brought me back to earth. I overprinted heavily on several titles, and they sold dismally. These setbacks frightened me into realizing how blindly I had been forging ahead, stumbling forward beneath the oppressive weight of an unhappiness whose source, given my outward success, seemed unidentifiable. I went to doctors, of course, but they could diagnose only the obvious — nervous depression brought on by physical exhaustion — and recommend I take four weeks of absolute rest and relaxation.

I took their advice and went to Capri. Why Capri? Because that was where Nicolas was. I could have taken the waters at Vichy in my beloved France, or sprawled on some sun-bleached Pacific island and danced under palm trees with nut-brown natives straight out of a Gauguin painting. But I didn't. My demons pushed me toward Nicolas — this other self, this drinker of my blood, this inhibitor of life.

How handsome he was in his house overlooking the ocean, my shining twin, how resplendent! He had chosen Capri for the azure of its sea and sky — and the beautiful models who paraded along the sides of the swimming pools, their breasts jiggling like so much ripe fruit waiting to be plucked. How could you blame him? How much more pleasant to sip Chianti in a dream landscape than to live, as I did, drowning lonely sorrows in a pint of warm ale in some musty urban pub.

There in Capri, surrounded by adorers and admirers, Nicolas reigned as supreme as a satrap. He was cock of the walk, imposing his whims, alternately playing the charmer and the sadistic prison warden for his guests. One morning while I was there he organized a walk along the beach, then for no apparent reason called it off an hour later. Poor Nicole, the pretty brunette who was his mistress of the hour. He would treat her like a slave one moment, shower her with flowers the next. He demanded absolute silence while he was writing, when he would sit at his desk and assume an exaggerated expression of concentration that I found truly exasperating.

Yet I couldn't help but envy Nicolas his magnetism, and his childish antics didn't seem to diminish it. He had preserved into adulthood intact the same luminous aura he had had when first I fell under his spell at the country club dance in Alexandria.

I knew I had no such aura. I was a nonentity, a cipher, absolutely devoid of charisma. What a cruel fate it is to be the sort of chap one might envy and yet not actually be able to see. To cross a room without notice and without remark. To be seated at a formal dinner party and wholly ignored by the people seated on either side. To be helpless, powerless, lifeless.

Sometimes I felt some essential part of me was missing, and that no matter how hard I tried, I would never find it. For example, it would frequently happen that I would go to a cocktail party and mix with the guests as energetically as I could. I would chivalrously kiss the hands of women and jovially slap the backs of men, join in conversations in every corner of the room, all the while munching lustily away on finger sand- wiches — in short doing everything possible to make myself noticed — only to hear someone ask me the very next day why I hadn't attended that very same party. Over the course of the years I must have held the door open for people more than a thousand times, gallantly insisted they go ahead of me into a store, onto an escalator, into a hotel. Yet never once did anyone ever thank me. Not that I can remember.

Why is it that while wandering lost in a foreign city one inevitably chooses another dazed tourist from whom to ask directions? Because colorless people are as neutral as a highway marker: looked at, passed by, forgotten. That is precisely how I felt. Some are born to a place among the gods, their arrival on earth at- tended by fairies. No such guiding spirit of greatness stood over my crib and blessed me. Life was the sta- tions of the cross, an upward climb toward inevitable doom. I trudged along as if atoning for some crime. What crime it was I couldn't even say.

Though I was talented at it, publishing had been the wrong profession for me. Gray and self-effacing, I was tailor-made for the secret service. Not only did I enjoy the advantage of transparency, I knew what it meant to lead a double life. Indeed, I had always known. Sir Edward Destry was a man with deep op- positions. Within me lived two souls — one that could function perfectly reasonably, if unobtrusively, in soci- ety; the other secretive, retreating into the cobwebbed corners of the subconscious to lick wounds that would never heal.

Nonetheless I was convinced it was this latter figure, this thing of pathos within, that embodied what genius nature had endowed me with. I was obsessed with the notion that it was Nicolas who had dispossessed me of my gifts, who had turned my genius into a reclusive, sulking caricature of what it might otherwise have been. Nicolas had stolen my life. Nothing short of that. I watched him closely in Capri, equally fascinated and tormented by jealousy, as he flaunted his abilities like a rich and spoiled child with a toy no one else can afford.

Nicolas's talents, I admit, could produce amusing results. But what they could have produced had I been master of them instead! His childish impulse to shock people, his need to punctuate his speech with vulgar expressions, his aggressiveness, his macho treatment of women. All so jejune. I would have done better.

His tantrums could also afford me bitter joy. Sometimes a wave of tenderness for him would overwhelm me. When he made one of his comically ferocious facial expressions, it reminded me of an illustrated encyclopedia I used to look at as a boy, in which there was a picture of a sultan murdering the messenger of bad news in a fit of rage.

I still believe that had Nicolas ever shown me any real consideration, all would have been forgiven. I would have been as happy as a dog praised by its master. That was it — I had always been waiting for Nicolas to stroke me. How I wanted to believe that his magisterial indifference was nothing but a facade, that he secretly rejoiced in my company! But he never gave me such a sign. Despite the years of our friendship, the memories that bound us together, and the favors that I had done for him, he treated me little better than he might someone with whom he had once eaten dinner. I was invisible to him as well. Once, over breakfast, I was passing him the toast, and he glanced at me. "Oh," he said, "it's you."

Yes, it was me. Me, the flower vase sitting on a corner of mantelpiece. The one you'd stopped looking at ages ago.

That small phrase — "Oh, it's you" — stirred deep anger. Damn you, Nicolas, I thought. It *is* me.

At least I was there enough for his son Peter, with whom over the years I had spent a great deal of time. Peter confided in me. Whenever his father, occupied elsewhere with his women or his parties, ignored him, it was to me the boy would come seeking solace. Each time Nicolas scolded him over something trivial, Peter and I were brought closer together. Even the invisible man can win the love of a child, after all, by listening to him and loving him with constancy and giving him presents and tucking him into bed at night. I learned all sorts of things about his father, though that was not why I did it. What I did for Peter was without thought of reward, but from love. He was the son I never had.

It pleased me that Peter loved me more than he did his father, and even more that this was a source of pain to Nicolas. Of course, out of pride, he willed himself not to reveal that pain to anyone. Yet I knew it was there.

I also secretly rejoiced when Nicolas experienced

writer's block. It happened several times during my stay on Capri. I watched with deep satisfaction as it drove him to distraction. He paced in circles like a caged wild animal, until finally he closed himself off from the world and drank. How my self-confidence and happiness soared! When Nicolas felt empty, I felt fulfilled. That was the seed of my conviction that his loss of creative energies would bring mine to life.

The last dry spell he hit was by far the longest, and it chanced to come toward the end of my visit. Nicolas could barely rouse himself to grumble good-bye to me, and I arrived in London feeling more at peace with myself than I had in years. I hoped his wretchedness would last.

Then one day, some months later, I received a letter from him, telling me that things had turned around. He was writing again, writing, he said, as he never had before.

"Something truly original and profound is stirring within. It may have been going on for years, but I have taken notice of its existence only recently. I am about to finish writing what I believe is a truly great novel."

He was as good as his word.

Never will I forget the day he brought his completed manuscript to me. It was entitled, *Il faut aimer.* A simpleminded title, I thought — "The Need to Love," roughly — but I knew straightaway it was unlike anything else he'd done. He had called me early that morning to tell me he had only just finished it, and that he was going to hop on a plane for London and personally place it in my hands.

At around two in the afternoon he marched into my office, without even taking the time to flirt with Doris. He was, I was surprised to see, trembling and looking abashed, like an aspiring novelist on a visit to an editor. At first I thought that something must be seriously wrong. The look on his face frightened me.

"Is anything the matter? Is Peter all right?" I asked in genuine alarm.

"Peter is fine. Here is the manuscript."

"Why show it to me first?" I asked. "Why not Laurent?"

"Your opinion is the one I'm after." Then he began to flatter me. I was the only one who could relieve him of his uncertainty as to how good it was. My nose for literary quality was better than anyone else's, whether the work was written in English or in French.

"You have all the right instincts," he concluded. "This is very different from my other work, Edward. The manuscript could mean a new beginning for me. How long will it take you to read it?"

"I don't know. A few hours, I suppose."

"Fine. I'll come by to get you this evening for a drink. In the meantime I'll go out for a walk."

It began creeping over me on page three — the slow-dawning feeling of horror. By the end of the first chapter I was fully enmeshed in a nightmare. The novel had a tragic heroine, a young Arab girl. Her name was Farida, but I knew instantly who she really was. My

Yasmina. Her eyes, her body, her tattoos, her laugh, the rags always slipping off her shoulder. Jealousy and rage attended every page, and the further I delved into the story, of Farida's seduction by a European, the more a black pain surged up from the very depths of my being. The creature within me was howling in agony.

It was too much to bear! With lovingly explicit descriptions of passion, Nicolas spread before the reader the intimate rites of initiation into a physical love so powerful and so cruel it bordered on the sordid, but somehow without losing a redeeming poignancy.

Farida's — Yasmina's — seducer, I knew, was Nicolas. It had to be. No one else could have invented this story. The evidence was overwhelming. Yasmina had been working as a maid in his house. He had gotten her pregnant. He was responsible for her death. Nicolas. No one else. Not me.

I raised my eyes from the manuscript and stared into a darkening corner of my office. For thirty years I had been consumed by guilt — a guilt that had sapped my will, my virility, my love of life itself. And for no reason. I understood the blind rage of Esau, deprived by deceit of the birthright that had been his. All Esau was left with was impotent rage at what the handsome and clever Jacob had taken from him.

The countless affronts accumulated over all those years had led to this greatest of all defilements: Nicolas had pillaged the dearest memory of my youth, Yasmina, and his manuscript, though stunningly beautiful, desecrated all that I had held most precious.

I had to read to the end. Wretchedly, I gripped each page with white knuckles while it seared itself onto my mortal soul. Had Nicolas been standing before me I know I would have killed him on the spot, ripped out his vital organs with my own hands.

Then at last I finished. The blind rage subsided. From the same deep well of my suffering came the conviction that I must restrain myself from physical violence, forced though I had been to watch while my youthful illusions were dashed unmercifully. The throb of hate and the ache for vengeance gained in depth and focus what they lost in virulence.

The tenor of my thoughts turned Machiavellian, subtlety distilled, calm.

The revelation that Nicolas was responsible for Yasmina's death exposed the true nature of all that resentment I had felt for him, all those years. Thirty years. By locating the source I also found the strength to channel it. As I look back now I see how necessary this act of discipline was. Do we not all inhabit a world of murders uncommitted, assassinations thwarted only by threat of justice? Were it otherwise, stories of spouses shooting each other would be routine, tales of butlers slitting the throats of their employers not even merit mention in a newspaper.

Physical violence was not possible. I was no longer a young man, and thank God for that. The callow young imbecile who had buried his passions in Egyptian catacombs had become a mature man of the world — blasé, experienced, and dangerous. A man capable of avenging himself without having to justify his reasons. I resolved to deal ruthlessly and in proportion with the wrongs I had suffered. How exactly, I had as yet absolutely no idea. I did know that I needed to strike Nicolas at his most vulnerable spot: the very manuscript I was reading.

The swirl of my emotions had not blinded me to the fact that it was indeed Nicolas's chef d'oeuvre, and that very likely it would give him what he craved: a new life. It would establish the name Nicolas Fabry among the first ranks of world-class writers. The subject was moving, new, the style more controlled and forceful than in his earlier works. Somehow Nicolas had succeeded in soaring above his past and given life, true and sincere life, to the wonderstruck adolescent he had always pretended not to be. He had flung off the mask of indifference and revealed himself in all his glory.

From that moment on, I was hypnotized by one goal: to use his novel as the means of my revenge.

In the months that followed, I inhabited a somnambulistic state, immersed in a private world. How fortunate it was that I had ingrained habits; they permitted one part of me to lead an apparently normal life, while its double, imprisoned for so long, was plotting its escape.

The second Doris left the office, I sprinted over to the photocopier and, unobserved, made a copy of the manuscript. The act calmed me, gave me the feeling I had begun to do something, so that by the time Nicolas came to fetch me I was my usual phlegmatic self. I saw with what anxiety he looked at me, and I immediately reassured him.

"It is a tour de force," I said simply.

His expression of doubt and worry was transformed into one of elation. He spirited me off to the Savoy for dinner and, I must admit, treated me royally the entire evening. Later that night he caught a flight back to Paris, clutching his precious manuscript under his arm.

Chapter 8

That very night I began translating *Il faut aimer* into English. I knew exactly how I was going to go about it. My plan was to be as faithful as possible to the original, and to leave the setting and plot virtually untouched. I would, however, push the date of the action back twenty years, a process that meant culling any language that sounded, in English at any rate, too contemporary. I retained the names of the principal characters and of course didn't in the slightest tinker with their psychology or manner of expression. The only real liberty I took was, here and there, to work in some of the vocabulary and cadences of a writer by the name of C. Irving Brown — for reasons I shall explain. These additions were small, but very telling.

For two weeks, toiling feverishly through the night, I slowly brought Nicolas's ravishing love story to the English language, feeling that as I did so I was doing much more than merely translating; I was stealing Nicolas's phrases one by one, extracting them with indescribable pleasure. Though I slept barely an hour or two at most, I felt no fatigue. I was driven by the idea that I must pay Nicolas back in kind for what he had stolen from me and reclaim the spirit of which he had dispossessed me all these years. Acts of revenge are never tiring.

In retrospect, it seems incredible to me that these preliminaries were undertaken with such calm and so automatically, because before reading the manuscript I had not consciously formulated any concrete plan of action. But when the thought had become conscious, I realized that I had already gathered most of the ingredients I would need.

The first, I had found years earlier. When I bought Turner Press I had directed that all unused and unusable stock be stored in a warehouse, and among that stock were several reams of virgin paper. Archibald's inventory report indicated they were being kept "for old time's sake," and when I looked closely at them I could see why — the paper was of a quality that hadn't been used in trade presses for years. There wasn't much of it. I recalled Archibald's having told me that there wasn't enough for even a small print run.

Why I decided to keep the paper rather than simply burning it for taking up valuable space, I do not know. Perhaps out of some vague, superstitious loyalty.

I found the second ingredient in an old building into which I had moved the business after Archibald's death. In the basement I discovered a dusty old trunk, and inside the trunk a collection of binding materials:

marbled paper for endpapers, blank stock for use as flyleaves, blue binding canvas, cotton, and linen thread for sewing the signatures. More remnants of days past. Again, I kept them.

The third ingredient came a bit later.

Everyone has his hobbies, and for some many years mine has been collecting old literary reviews, particularly those that featured prewar writers. One day, while scanning a magazine called the *Sorcerer's Review*, I found a very impressive short story entitled "Whilst Albion Slept," written in the late 1930s by a C. Irving Brown. The name meant nothing to me. No one I asked seemed to have ever heard of him. Intrigued, I began to investigate this nearly anonymous writer, even though I knew nothing about him — whether he was from London or Liverpool, whether he'd been to college or not, whether he'd written other books. Absolutely nothing. All I had to go on was that one short piece. My intuition told me it showed signs of a significant talent. At the beginning of my hunt I was fairly confident that I should be able to locate him or other examples of his work without difficulty.

I was mistaken. No C. Irving Brown was listed in the catalog of the British Library, and his name appeared on no list of authors and no other prewar literary review. As for the *Sorcerer's Review*, it had disappeared altogether.

I was about to give up when an elderly book collector I happened to chat with gave me the address of a writer's association that, he believed, still had the archives of the review in question. I went over immediately, asked to see these archives, and there —

mirabile dictu — found the only extant proof of C. Irving Brown's existence. In a musty old folder, hidden among a number of business documents, was a calling card on which was printed

C. IRVING BROWN

133 Dickens Road

IPSWICH

I felt the joy a detective feels when finally he cracks a case. The game was afoot! I jumped in my car and sped over to Ipswich. Disappointment awaited. The name "Brown" appeared on none of the dozens of decrepit mailboxes located in the entryway of a singularly charmless apartment building.

My investigation came to a close at Ipswich City Hall, where I had gone to make a last-ditch inquiry with the registrar of births and deaths. What little he had been able to tell me seemed definitive enough.

"Chatterton Irving Brown, born February 23rd, 1917, died on June 1st, 1940, at Dunkirk. He was unmarried and childless."

"What about his parents?"

"Both deceased."

Such a shame, I thought. For all his promise, C. Irving Brown would not be immortalized by the Turner Press. Anyway, soon I began to forget all about him. It was shortly after reading Nicolas's manuscript that his name resurfaced.

The manner in which these disparate elements might work together occurred to me with the full force of an epiphany while driving home after my dinner at the Savoy with Nicolas. Lo, an answer had appeared unto me, and it was a demonically clever one. I would summon the spirit of the dead C. Irving Brown to exorcize from my soul forever the specter of Nicolas Fabry.

The minute I got home I began to construct, step by jubilant step, my plan.

I had a usable author. What I needed now was a publisher. In the days that followed I traipsed all over London learning what I could about publishing houses destroyed during the Blitz. I was after a small one, modest but literary, which had not published anything after its fiery demise. Naturally, I employed the greatest discretion. The very last thing I wanted to do was attract attention, even Doris's. I acted entirely on my own and delegated nothing.

Haunting the pubs along Fleet Street, I sought out the older veterans of English publishing, buying whiskeys to loosen their tongues but being careful not to arouse their suspicions. They were only too delighted to be given the chance to ramble on and on about the good old days, particularly to someone who hadn't known them and couldn't contradict their versions.

Eventually I succeeded in compiling a list of all the publishers that had disappeared between 1940 and 1945, noting the kinds of books they did. Then I went through all the secondhand bookstores in London, checking and cross-checking their collections. It was tedious and exacting work.

By the end of three weeks' hard labor I had settled

on a publishing house. Founded in 1937, Marble Arch Press had published only a few titles, and the print runs were very small, consisting mostly of works by promising young writers destined never to make a career of their writing. Bombing during the Blitz had decimated its offices, along with all the files and accounts, and it never recovered. Its sole owner and publisher, Philip Ramsay, had been killed late in the war during the Allies' Sicilian campaign.

All this suited my needs perfectly, but it was the manner in which Marble Arch had published books that guided my choice. The paper, casing material, and flyleaves were identical to the ones I already had in my possession.

Marble Arch Press had a very modest operating budget, and to save money Ramsay had used the services of several different printers, never establishing long-term relations with any one in particular. It was necessary to dig up a few books the press had published for examination, so I called on specialty bookshops around London, concentrating my efforts in Bloomsbury. In less than a fortnight I had uncovered three works. It was child's play to take them apart and analyze their assemblage.

Now began the real work. The summer internship I had spent working at a printer's shop twenty years ago on the advice of Archibald Turner proved enormously useful, for it had familiarized me with typesetting and printing. Even after all those years I had not forgotten about the monotypes that set up individual characters, or the linotypes that compose entire lines. Back then, though I couldn't pretend to compete with those professionals capable of typesetting 10,000 characters an hour, I had acquitted myself well.

The various printers used by Marble Arch Press worked with linotypes. This meant I needed to get my hands on some old equipment. After several weeks' search, I came across a small advertisement for a press in a professional review. The heirs of a recently deceased printer from Chester by the name of Peter Thyman were selling off exactly what I was looking for. Thyman's business had ended in bankruptcy, and the heirs had been forced to assume his debt. For a very modest sum they let me cart off a small press that did quarto printing and a linotype machine manufactured by Harris Intertype. They also threw in a complete set of classical Didot fonts, traditionally used in books published in England before 1939. I paid for everything in cash.

This gave me everything I needed to print my forgery. I transported my spoils to the garage of my summer house in Dorchester, there to do the deed.

I prepared for every contingency, devoted to each and every detail such punctilious attention as to border on manic obsessiveness. My perfectionism energized me, filled me with such malicious joy that I greeted every day with eager anticipation.

After some trial and error I managed to break down the composition of the natural glues prewar binders had used, then manufactured several flasks of the stuff. I also reconstituted ink from linseed oil, whose odor I remembered the instant I smelled it. Soon my garage was filled with everything required to print a dozen copies of a novel, roughly three hundred printed pages in length, bearing the name, colophon, and distinctive markings of Marble Arch Press.

I had allotted myself six months to get everything ready. Given how clean Nicolas's original manuscript was, I knew that Editions Millagard would probably bring the book out on a rushed schedule to qualify it for the next Goncourt Prize. I had to be ready. Timing was critical. Normally, since I had a multibook contract with Millagard, I was permitted to begin translation work on Nicolas's novels so that they might appear nearly simultaneously in English and in French, but this time Nicolas had insisted I wait until after the book's official French publication date. I didn't protest, since it gave me that much more time.

Employing the same perfectionist logic, I learned to compose several pages of linotype, line by line, until I found the leading to match the original. By now I was familiar with everything about Marble Arch Press books — house style, composition regularities, layout, location of ornaments, even their pagination.

So involved did I become with Philip Ramsay's old press that I almost completely ignored the Turner Press, and was forced to delegate most of the day-to-day operations to others. I still went to the office, of course, so as not to cause alarm, but my concentration was less than optimal. I knew this would be so. I also knew that as soon as my project was complete I would return to the Turner Press with redoubled enthusiasm and energy.

When all the preparatory work had been completed, I obtained a medical recommendation from my personal physician, Dr. Gorham, to refrain for reasons of health from all business activity. Getting this recommendation was not difficult. I may not have felt tired, but I looked an absolute wreck. Turner Press would simply have to get along without me for a couple of weeks.

With the well wishes of my staff (Doris with tears in her eyes), off I went to my country house and set to work immediately on the laborious process of typesetting Nicolas's novel. The work began to take form, and my technique improved. Naturally I couldn't go nearly as fast as an experienced typesetter, and with a magnifying glass I inspected every word after printing it. The detail involved did not diminish my ardor for the work. It was the same ardor I had felt during the war in those Dorchester bomb shelters, where we printed counterfeit orders for our colleagues behind enemy lines.

From the first half-title to the last line of *The Need to Love* (I had settled on this as the title of my translation), my attention never wandered. On the contrary, the whole experience enlarged my consciousness. Still, when I composed the final page, I must say it was with a certain sense of relief.

All that remained was to compose the traditional "Printed in Great Britain, by Peter Thyman Ltd., Chester." Prewar copyright laws were such that I was not compelled to mention either the publication date or the registration number. All I put was "First Edition, 1939."

No sooner had I finished with the composition

than I began actually printing, page by page, recto/ verso, the twelve copies that my supply of paper permitted.

However, the final element — the binding — I could not do by myself. I had decided that I would go to Egypt and have it done there. I was sure I would find a craftsman to put the final touches on my master-piece. Egypt had the immense advantage of being far away. Employing the services of a binder closer to hand could be dangerous.

Besides, I needed to get away. The work and the secrecy had taken rather a heavy toll, and it was not a good idea to return to the office looking like a corpse, particularly after two weeks of rustic life, which should have done me a world of good. A trip abroad would help me gather the strength I needed for the final offensive, and so abroad I went.

Chapter 9

I could probably have found a craftsman binder in Spain or elsewhere, but I thought Egypt's dry heat would help me to unwind. I felt no particular urge to go home again and made no plans to visit Alexandria. I had been back once since the death of my mother and found the experience deeply disappointing. I hadn't recognized the city that I had loved so much. A miserable populace groveled in dark, grimy corners, where in past days a cosmopolitan crowd paraded through the streets. Our old house had been torn down, and a grotesquely somber apartment building constructed in its place. Even the Pastrodis was gone, another victim to time and the bulldozer.

Instead I flew to Cairo with suitcases rather too heavy for a one-week tourist visit, stuffed with everything necessary for the fabrication of a dozen volumes of *The Need to Love.* The rest was hidden in a shed at my country house.

I hired a car at Cairo airport to get around more freely, and early the next morning, with addresses furnished by the telephone directory, I set out to visit some dozen binderies. Those that looked too filthy to do a careful enough job or too large to be discreet I instantly eliminated, without even bothering to check whether they had the right machinery. After a full day of crisscrossing the city, I finally found an elderly Arab binder who spoke neither English nor French. His shop was located near the souk, on Sidi-Metwalli street. Modest but well maintained, it seemed an oasis of order in the heart of the old city. More to the point, he had all the old machines necessary to do the kind of semimechanical binding common in the prewar period in Europe. Yet another stroke of fate.

I still spoke Arabic effortlessly, and at first the old boy was a bit taken aback by a European who could speak in the Egyptian dialect, and fluently at that. I explained I had spent most of my youth in Egypt, then got directly to the point. He acceded to my demands and didn't seem at all surprised that I would provide all the materials — the backing, the paper, the canvas, threads, even the glue. It is part of the established wisdom of the Orient that Westerners, and in particular the British, are eccentric to the point of derangement. Naturally, that is no reason to turn away their business.

After repeating all my requests many more times than was necessary, I left him to his work, telling him that I would return in three days to pick the books up. To ensure his goodwill and show my good faith I paid him a portion of what I would owe him. I could see that he was fully capable, and, my spirit lightened, I flew that same evening to Aswan.

The dry heat of the Upper Nile offered a respite from the oppressive humidity of Cairo. I spent hours on end sitting on the balcony of my room at the Old Cataract Hotel, watching the iridescent river wash over the rocks of Elephantine Island. The ruins of Alexander II's Ptolemaic temple stood in majestic profile against the embracing sky, while the giant sails of the felouks glided silently by, their wake lapping quietly against the blocks of rose granite. In the freshness of the evening I let myself be seduced by the perfumes that ascended to me and by the subtle alliance of odors of rosebushes and orange trees. This magnificent and serene country, reconquered by my grandfather at the side of the great Kitchener himself, relaxed and replenished me. I even think that during the three days I spent there, Nicolas Fabry did not once cross my mind. After so many gray, solitary years, I was feeling reborn into the world.

I awoke at dawn and hired a felouk to take me up the Nile to the dam. By means of both oars and sails, two Nubian boatmen maneuvered the vessel through the rapids with great agility, pushing off against the glistening and dangerous rocks with their long poles and chanting to help their efforts. I watched sunlight revealing the bas-reliefs and hieroglyphics carved into the corridors of granite through which we were passing. In the distance I could hear the roar of the great falls, and from the edges of the river, the creaking wheels of the *sakkiehs* being turned by slow-moving water buffalo in harness. That morning light, with its bluish transparency, was not new to me, but the sights it illuminated had changed. Several of the monuments had been removed from the banks to prevent them from being submerged when Nasser raised the height of the dam. One could no longer enter by boat into the flooded gates of the temple of Isis on the island of Philae, where the effigies of the gods greeted the visitor at eye level. Everything was different. Rather than the lapping of tiny ripples, one heard a distant rumble.

I returned to the hotel dazzled and nostalgic. The unbearable tension of the past few months was dissolving. The air-conditioning in the lobby made me shiver. The elevator operator's smile, however, was very warm.

"Does sir want a whiskey in his room?" he inquired in uncertain English.

He had the fine features and elongated elegance of a Nubian. His long white galabia, fastened around his slim waist by a large garnet-colored belt, made his skin seem darker, so dark that you would almost have said it was violet. We were alone in the elevator, and I had just spent several weeks living in ascetic isolation from the world. I asked him what time he got off work.

"Right away, sir," he replied with a second, even grander smile.

"In that case, I should be very pleased if you would bring me a bottle of Scotch, some ice, and two glasses," I said as I was getting off the elevator.

Several minutes later he knocked at my door, balancing a tray on the delicate fingertips of his left hand. Clearly this was not the first time he had spent a few off-duty hours with a client passing through. But his manner combined natural dignity with a sincere desire to please, and our little time together never fell into the vulgarity of a paid embrace. The following evening he again knocked on my door, with the same smile devoid of either arrogance or false solicitude.

Dappled walks in the gardens along the banks of the Nile, under the sycamores and flame trees. Tender nights of passion. The three days I spent in Aswan floated in a different time, and I deeply regretted it was only three. I needed to return to Cairo to pick up my books and plunge back into my hellish plot.

The binder had ample reason to be proud of his work: the twelve volumes conformed to my instructions down to the last detail.

I flipped through the pages, immediately absorbed by the need to hold between my own two hands the means of my revenge, to gauge the authenticity of its deadliness. My hand trembled; it was perfect. Everything was there to create an unimpeachable illusion — the cover, the paper, the type, even the feel of the pages turning between my thumb and index finger. The forgery had all the earmarks (should I say bookmarks?) of legitimacy.

Having paid the old binder the remainder of what he was due and showered him with baksheesh to ensure his silence, I flew back that same evening to London. I got through customs, found my car in the airport, and headed straight for my country house. My books needed their finishing touches.

I stacked eight copies together, then bound them with twine, putting the ones that had small defects on the top and bottom. Then, with the disagreeable feeling that I was committing auto-da-fé, I built a large fire in the fireplace, feeding it with the paper and cardboard that was left over.

All this was done with the solemnity of a religious ritual. I was purifying by fire the work of my life and by so doing commending Nicolas to it.

A glass of Scotch in one hand, I waited for the fire to die down. When it had become a tapestry of glowing coals, I threw in the parcel of books and then, for two interminable minutes, I waited. When the trial by fire was over I dumped a bucket of water on the coals and retrieved the books. The two volumes at either end were in ruins, half burned, blackened, and soggy. But the six in the middle were only singed and slightly soiled by soot and water. Carefully, I removed them and placed them to dry on a radiator.

A little dust, lovingly collected from my basement, was rubbed on the six copies, which were subjected to a prolonged session under ultraviolet light to give them their patina.

At last I held in my hands the six remaining copies of *The Need to Love,* a novel by C. Irving Brown, published in 1939 by the Marble Arch Press.

My work was finished. The next day I would return to the Turner Press, where everyone would compliment me on how wonderfully rested I looked. Several days after that I would go to three bookstores I had selected and quietly slip a copy onto the shelves, like so many messages in a bottle. The other three would be securely stowed in my safe to await their moment.

As I had predicted, nearly the minute his book was published Nicolas had become the toast of Paris. *Il faut aimer*'s success was immediate and total, critical as well as commercial, and like a strong spirit drunk too fast, it had intoxicated Nicolas. He had, however, taken the trouble to write from the South of France and tell me that my original estimation had once again proven correct.

> Weather in Cannes is beautiful. Sun and glorious sea. I have never had such incredible reviews. My god, Edward! Curiosity, passion, hyperbole, and furor all commingled at the launching of my book. My oldest enemies are following suit, even if they are also taking advantage of their newfound enthusiasm to excoriate one more time all my old work. Everyone is praising to the skies the originality of style and tone, stunned that after such a long and mediocre career I might be capable of such talent —
> I can breathe!
> Overnight I have become a writer newborn. I have been waiting for this for twenty years, waiting to erase forever the image that hounded me after my first bestseller. I am delivered of my arrogance, and I understand, deeply and truly, the meaning of artistic humility. I am at peace with myself, happy, and, for the first time in my life, satisfied —

This simple, unaffected letter should have touched me, perhaps, but all I could read between the lines was false sincerity. Nicolas's hold over me had been irrevocably weakened the moment I had begun my revenge. Day after day, as my design took shape and form, a process of exorcism was occurring, a weaning process that little by little was liberating me from this perversely brilliant man.

No, it was too late. I would not be taken in. I had closed the book on that part of my life forever.

Chapter 10

Rain drenched Heathrow Airport, and taxis were impossible to find. I was exhilarated.

Black skies were good signs.

I believed in portents then. I shivered at crossed silverware and read into the flight patterns of swallows. Knocking over the salt shaker was cause for panic. I fretted over the Ides of March and umbrellas opened indoors and the idea of walking under a ladder.

The fate of Caius Flaminius came often to mind. At Lake Trasimene he had foolishly engaged his enemy in battle despite a formal warning from his oracles that the signs were not auspicious; he was defeated and then executed by Hannibal.

Doris had put flowers on my desk. I opened the door, and she looked as if she might throw herself into my arms. Thankfully, this did not happen. She greeted me effusively, then blushed and told me, with the look of a naughty child, that there was a bottle of champagne in my office refrigerator.

"Well, you see, to celebrate the success of — and, well, because Mr. Fabry's success is in part because of you and me, I thought . . ."

Sweet Doris. She thought of everything. There she was, loyal as ever, ready to share in my joy. I couldn't bear to cause her any pain.

"Indeed, Doris! Indeed! What do you say we just open it up then?" I replied in my jauntiest voice. She beamed with pleasure.

We toasted the success of Nicolas Fabry, and we toasted the happy fact that the Turner Press owned English-language rights to his book (part of a multi-book deal I had signed with him ages back), and that that would mean yet another resounding success for us. I told her about my trip to Paris, the cocktails at Millagard's, the evening at Castel's, Nicolas's ecstasies, Nora's beauty. . . . But I said nothing about my little adventure with the chubby Margot. She shuddered when I told her about the return flight and turned pale, and I saw how it touched her. How different life would have been had I simply been in love with Doris.'

Then she hinted that I must have quite a few things to catch up on, and that perhaps she should leave me for a while. She withdrew, discreet as ever.

Dear Marianne Evans:

My admiration for your critical acuity and my respect for your professional honesty lead me to conclude that you are the only person with whom I would share the very deep distress I felt reading the acclaimed new French novel entitled *Il faut aimer* by the French writer Nicolas Fabry. . . .

My hand was steady as I composed the letter, using a typewriter I had bought especially for the purpose. On a single sheet of paper, without letterhead, I explained my shock at the "extraordinary and surely not coincidental similarities between Nicolas Fabry's novel and C. Irving Brown's 1939 work, *The Need to Love*, a copy of which I enclose." They were more than happenstance could explain, I wrote, adding that I was positive she would find Brown's novel truly edifying.

I ended by explaining that I was an elderly and retired professor of French, who preferred his identity to remain unknown.

I sealed the thick brown envelope.

The time bomb was set. Now it was up to Ms. Evans to detonate it. I was sure she would do so with pleasure. Few people on earth despised Nicolas Fabry more heartily than Marianne Evans.

I had introduced them three years earlier at a cocktail party in London. Never would I have thought her the type to fall for Nicolas. A career journalist, she was committed to her ambitions, to money and glory. Moreover, at the time she was having a no doubt very useful fling with the editor-in-chief of the newspaper in which her intelligently written though sharply barbed book reviews appeared with regularity. I would have thought her capable of anything *except* allowing herself to be devoured by a paper tiger like Nicolas. Yet that same evening Evans met Nicolas at his hotel room, and the next morning, rather publicly, she ended her affair with the editor.

It was a very stupid thing to do. Why get caught

up in an affair of the heart in which within a matter of days one participant would be incapable of providing any emotional satisfaction? Nicolas dumped Marianne five days later and went home to his mistress in Paris.

She never quite recovered from it. You could tease her about anything except her vanity. From that day onward she systematically decimated any work of Fabry's the day it appeared.

I was giving her a wonderful occasion for revenge.

I stayed late at the office, then went and dropped the envelope in Marianne's mailbox on the other side of London.

It was something of a miracle that I managed to get home without an accident. I drove mindlessly, not sure of where I was going, nor even who I was.

That first night I slept very little, drifting in and out of a twilight dreamland peopled by moving shadows. Several times I became absolutely convinced that someone was in the room with me, whispering. Apparitions of my anxiety, I knew. Finally I lulled myself to sleep by reminding myself over and over that the man I had condemned was guilty a thousand times over, that my revenge was poetic justice. And how bad could it be, really? All I was doing was throwing a spanner in the works — hoping to spook Nicolas just a bit, instill in him a fear of some nameless foe. Good God, the man deserved at least that.

The three days that followed seemed interminable. I barricaded myself in my office, waiting for a reaction, unable to concentrate, asking that no one interrupt me for any reason. The one thing that I did manage to accomplish, with a very clear mind, was research (done very discreetly, of course) into the rights to the Marble Arch Press book. Having invented an author, a publisher, and a book, if I also wanted to publish *The Need to Love* at some point later on, I would still have to acquire the rights. I traced the descendants of Philip Ramsay. One relative was still alive. He worked in a bank. I noted down his exact whereabouts, promising myself that when the moment came I would move more quickly than my competitors and obtain the rights — to the work of which I was the creator.

When I think back, aspects of my plot can still make me feel dizzy.

Finally, it happened. And it went exactly as I had hoped. Marianne Evans published a piece in the *Times* entitled "The Prize of Plagiarism." In it she loudly denounced Nicolas Fabry's astounding duplicity for having recopied in extenso a prewar English novel, doubtless counting on the idea that its true author, C. Irving Brown, would be nearly unknown even in his native land. What irony it was that the work of an unknown British writer had won its French plagiarist the most prestigious award his country could bestow, the Goncourt!

Evans noted that it was only by the most incredible stroke of luck that she had been able to get her hands on a copy of the original *The Need to Love.* Otherwise a true masterpiece might have remained forever unknown, and the outrageous perfidy of its imitator gone undiscovered.

The case of the "Fabry Fabrication" took wing. I was sitting at my desk, reading and rereading Evans's article, when a quiet knock at my door drew me out of my reverie. Doris informed me that Millagard was on the line and that he absolutely insisted on being put through.

"He sounds extremely upset," she said.

Trying very hard not to smile, I picked up the phone. Millagard was indeed in a full panic. He had just been told about the article in the *Times*. What was all this nonsense? He said I must write a letter to the *Times,* that very moment, summarily denouncing Evans's libelous charges. I replied, coolly, that it would be better to find out everything we could before acting.

"I would say nothing to Nicolas for the moment," I advised him.

"Edward, come right away. Immediately."

I told him I would be on the next plane for Paris.

My Parisian colleagues were in an uproar. Word of Evans's accusation had leaked. Employees were running in every direction, telephones were going off like alarms. In Millagard's office a "crisis meeting" had been convened. The house solicitor was there, going over the article in the *Times* with a translator to make absolutely certain he understood the full meaning of every single word.

Millagard greeted me as the Messiah. Instructing the secretary to leave them, he grabbed the copy of the *Times* the lawyer had been reading and begged me to translate the article out loud. He was clinging to the hope that my rendition might be different from the others. A religious silence prevailed while I read. Everyone in the room held their breath.

When I had finished, I folded the newspaper, placed it on the table, and turned to Millagard with a look that I could only hope successfully masked the joy leaping inside me.

"It's a low blow," I said lamely. "Does anyone here think for one second that Nicolas would be capable of such a thing?"

"I — I can't say. I honestly know absolutely nothing. The whole thing is so — so incredible! Edward, what are we going to do?"

"A journalist like Marianne Evans can't afford to make something like this up," I replied evenly. "In any event, we have to get in touch with Nicolas right away."

"He's already been told. But what can we do? What is to be done?" Millagard looked despairingly at the solicitor.

"We should start by intimidating our adversary," the solicitor, a man named Joly, replied. "Later we can offer our proof of Fabry's innocence. We need to make it clear we will do everything we can to clear our name. Our reputation is at stake, after all."

If the miserable Millagard hadn't been so shaken himself, he would have probably throttled Joly.

"Thank you! I know that!" he roared. "But how can we attack this Evans without any facts? Only Nicolas . . ."

Millagard had barely uttered his name when the author himself burst into the office. He was disheveled, unshaven, his face contorted by a rage so intense that it twisted his lips.

This vision of him did me a world of good. I had never seen him so unraveled. He was sputtering with indignation and struggling for words.

"Nicolas! What is all this about? Tell us!" demanded Millagard.

Nicolas collapsed on the couch, mumbling incoherently. I thought it possible he might have a nervous breakdown right there.

"I've — I've — I've been framed," he managed.

"By whom?" thundered Millagard.

"By Evans! Who else? The bitch hates me. If this thing" — he couldn't bring himself to say "book" — "exists, then she's the one who wrote it. But it won't work! No, by God!"

He sat upright. Color came back to his face.

"Have you filed suit?" asked Joly.

"Of course I have! I'm asking that you take charge of the case immediately." His voice was gaining back some of its authority.

"Nicolas," I said, "this is a very serious business for us all, and we must act in unison. You have to tell us honestly whether you knew about this book, and if, even unconsciously, it might have influenced you when you were writing."

He looked at me with the eyes of a condemned

man being led to the scaffold. "No, I swear to you. Never."

He leaned over and covered his face with his hands.

At that moment Millagard's secretary stuck her head in to say that there were some journalists outside, insisting on an interview. Word was spreading fast.

Publisher and lawyer looked at each other, then both began to shrug their shoulders — as the French do — but in such mechanical and rapid succession that they reminded me of characters out of Lewis Carroll. I could barely keep from laughing. Nicolas hadn't moved and made no sound. He seemed to be in a different world.

"Tell them to wait," I said to the secretary, indicating that she should withdraw.

I turned toward Millagard.

"We need to get Nicolas out of here without anybody seeing him. He's in no condition to talk to journalists. It would be best for him to lay low for a few days. At least until we have a clearer picture. You and I will face the press."

Monsieur Joly led — carried, really — Nicolas into a connecting office, and Millagard and I went out and called in the journalists who had been pacing impatiently in the hallway. They didn't even bother waiting for the door to close behind them before they started shooting out questions. They knew the *Times* article by heart and demanded to know how we answered its charges. An auctioneer couldn't have sifted through their shouts. Stunned by the verbal violence, Millagard went white. I had to come to his rescue and calm them as best I could.

"Please, now, please, ladies and gentlemen, PLEASE," I shouted. "I must ask you to listen carefully to what I am about to say. Before Ms. Evans's article, I for one had never heard of C. Irving Brown, and I am something of an expert in contemporary British fiction, in addition to being the very proud publisher of the works of Nicolas Fabry. In England there is a catalog of the works of every British writer going back to the eighteenth century. I would be interested to know if the name C. Irving Brown appears anywhere in it. Before echoing any accusations about Nicolas Fabry, I strongly suggest you verify your sources and not assume that Ms. Evans's vengeful article contains the truth. She might have made the whole thing up."

A cold silence greeted my words, but I pressed ahead. "At this stage, we know little more than you. As soon as we have any concrete evidence, Monsieur Millagard and I will organize a press conference, to which you will of course all be invited. I will only remind each of you that, starting this very moment, we will consider any accusation made against Monsieur Fabry — until there is any proof — as defamation, and act accordingly."

Realizing they would get nothing more from us, the journalists filed out and retreated back to their papers to begin writing their copy. It wasn't every day that a scoop of this importance landed on their doorstep.

I looked at Millagard. He was staring at his office door as if at any moment it might fly open again and the nightmare recommence. I asked his secretary to bring him a glass of water and dialed my solicitor, Sir Charles Vanderon.

Vanderon's advice was that before we could bring suit against Evans and the *Times,* we should obtain an expert opinion verifying that *The Need to Love* was a fraud. Once we had that, the panic would subside. There would be all the time in the world to bring a civil suit for libel and defamation of character.

I told him to get on it immediately.

Then Millagard and I together composed an announcement in the name of both Turner Press and Editions Millagard, unequivocally stating our support of Nicolas Fabry. It would, we knew, be picked up by every major newspaper in both London and Paris.

Nicolas had rejoined us after the departure of the journalists and was pacing around the office, alternately silent and shouting. When I told him I was leaving for London that evening, he screamed, "I'm coming with you! I'm going to kill that slut!"

He was nearly foaming at the mouth.

"No, Nicolas," replied Millagard, who had regained his composure. "You must stay here. Leaving would be interpreted as an admission of guilt."

"Laurent's absolutely correct," I chimed in. "The last thing you want to do is look as if they can make you run."

"But I'm innocent! Don't you understand?"

His tone carried the ring of sincerity, and that made it all the more pitiful.

"This is precisely why you must not leave," said Millagard, standing up. "Innocent people do not run. Save your strength, my friend. What we've just faced is nothing compared to what's coming next. You're going to have to confront them eventually."

Nicolas hung his head and was silent. Millagard gave him a look in which I thought I could read a bitterness that bordered on hatred.

I left them there. I needed to get back to London to stoke the fire that, when it had burned out, would have reduced the life of Nicolas Fabry to smoldering ruins.

Everything about my flight back seemed to augur well — the azure of the sky, the fluffy shapes of the clouds, even the pilot's assured voice. I let myself become absorbed by the newspapers' accounts of what was now universally being termed the "Fabrycation Affair." The papers had no new information to provide, though some of them, not content with simply parroting the same news, elaborated on the myth of Nicolas Fabry, that successful writer of fiction whose career seemed threatened with scandal and disaster at the very moment when his latest work was enjoying enormous critical success. Some offered limited speculation about C. Irving Brown, unknown even in his native land.

I savored every word and every line of every article, and with a delicious sense of vanity, because most journalists were repeating Marianne Evans's estimation that the original English version was far better than the French fraud. The days ahead, I suspected, would bring me even more accolades. C. Irving Brown would be the uncrowned winner of the Goncourt

Prize. I would be the only one to appreciate what I had achieved.

I was already beginning to sense a new appetite for things. Dull roots were stirring. I felt less unprepossessing, as if my colorless soul were starting to flush with life.

I asked the flight attendant for a Scotch and further indulged myself by giving her an undressing look. She acknowledged it and smiled coquettishly. Then I stretched out my legs and sipped the whiskey. How long it had been since I had felt such intoxication, such sweet euphoria!

I got to my office in London still feeling ebullient. Doris was frantically fielding phone calls. They were coming in from all over — readers, reviewers, journalists, even authors. Everyone was getting the news, and as Fabry's British publisher and longtime friend, I was the one they were calling for details. I ordered the switchboard shut down and gathered the entire staff in the large conference room.

"We are not the principals in this business," I declared. "It is true we have been Nicolas Fabry's publisher since the beginning, but for the moment, and until there has been some resolution or further elaboration, we will remove his latest work from our forthcoming list. Each one of you must understand how critical it is that we keep our composure in the face of what is at best mere presumption of guilt. I am relying on all of you."

Not a memorable speech, but it had its desired effect in calming the troops.

Two hours later I called Millagard to tell him what

I had been able to discover. I confirmed that C. Irving Brown's work had indeed not been cataloged in the British Museum, but added, trying not to sound malicious, that in England it was customary not to register a book until the moment it was shipped to booksellers. Given the date of publication, it was quite possible that the Marble Arch Press had been unable to register the book before their offices were destroyed by the German bombing. As for Brown himself, he was not to be found in the registry of authors at the British Library, and was thought to have published only one short piece in a defunct review called *The Sorcerer's Review*.

"That's the only trace we have of his writing," I concluded. "However, I'm afraid that it proves that he really did exist. I'm sorry, Laurent."

"We are in a shithole! A shithole!"

"Do let's keep our heads. We have to wait for the expert opinion being sought by John Holland."

"Our lawyers don't agree on this, Edward. Nicolas has already filed suit."

"A regrettable mistake, Laurent. Extremely regrettable. But since both men seem sure of what they're doing, we'll have to wait for the trial."

In my heart of hearts, I was delighted by Nicolas's decision to go to court. Wanting to take the initiative, solicitors would force the issue, and that would mean that everything would come to a head even faster than I had ever dreamed possible. The career of Nicolas Fabry was hanging by a thread.

The following morning, the BBC invited me to appear on television. I took the opportunity to reiterate, very reasonably I thought, that there was a considerable difference between accusation and guilt. *The Need to Love* could still very well turn out to be a forgery, and we would simply have to wait for the experts' conclusions. I requested that the British press not use this occasion to open old wounds with our friends the French.

To the question, "Do you or do you not intend to publish the English translation of *Il faut aimer*?" I replied that only formal proof of Fabry's guilt would keep me from doing so.

There was nothing to do but wait.

Chapter 11

On the eve of the hearing, I went out to Heathrow to pick up Millagard and Nicolas. Both looked as if they'd aged ten years. I was pleased to note that Nicolas had developed a facial tic — a little muscle in his left cheek twitched incessantly, giving the impression that he was winking at you.

From the same plane emerged numerous members of the French press corps — editors, reviewers, commentators of every ideological stripe. And among them was my pudgy conquest Margot Zembla, stuffed into a dress covered with spangles. Her hair was a brilliant red and her lips deep purple. She looked a horror. Persuaded that I had come expressly to welcome her, she launched herself directly at me, making a symphony of endearing noises. I recoiled in embarrassment. Once she realized that I had come to welcome Nicolas, I thought things might turn ugly, so I quickly invited her to dine with me the following day. Best to make no enemies, I thought. One never knows.

It had been years since the Old Bailey had seen such a crowd. The press had done everything it could to create a sensation. Not a day went by in which at least one major article on Nicolas was not featured prominently. So far, denouncing him had brought nothing but glory to Marianne Evans. Indeed, it was impossible to talk about one without mentioning the other, particularly when the details of their brief affair were being recirculated and her notoriety had reached vertiginous heights.

The court was packed. Literary celebrities, actors, journalists, and of course the entirety of the London press corps — plus hundreds of the simply curious. Nicolas's arrival was greeted with exclamations. He looked superb, I must say, in his conservative pin-striped suit, but his expression was tense.

Marianne Evans had preceded him into the room, sumptuously draped in a sort of beige dress-coat combination. Accused and accuser barely exchanged a glance. Nicolas took his place on the bench next to Millagard. Beside them an English solicitor nervously riffled through some documents. Soon enough, the bailiff announced that the court was in session, and all rose while the bewigged judge made his sweeping entrance up the stairs to his cathedra. He solemnly read the accusation of plagiarism and turned to Nicolas's solicitor to ask how his client responded.

"If it please the court, Your Honor," replied the solicitor with animation, "I would remind you that we are defendants at a hearing, not respondents at an indictment. It is rather for Miss Evans to defend her reckless charges."

The judge's face, already florid from years of sherry and port consumption, I suspected, reddened further, and he gave the solicitor a withering look, then turned his attention to Marianne Evans.

"Miss Evans," he said, peering down over his reading glasses. "Can you enlighten me as to on what basis you are bringing this accusation against Monsieur Fabry?"

Marianne inclined her head, upon which was tilted a wide-brimmed silk hat, and waited before responding. It was clear she intended to savor her moment of glory to the fullest. She was well aware of the effect her appearance had on the spectators.

"Your Honor, I have brought with me," she said, "tangible proof that the novel by Mr. Fabry, recently published in France, is a plagiarism. I have handed over the work from which Mr. Fabry did his version for expert evaluation. The work in question is a novel, entitled *The Need to Love,* written by C. Irving Brown. By making this known to the public I have only done my duty as a journalist, and not engaged, as Mr. Fabry's lawyers would have you believe, in vindictive and defamatory behavior. These experts were agreed to by both parties, and I think it would be best if we turn to their testimony as quickly as possible."

"The experts will be heard in due time, Miss Evans," replied the judge.

"Certainly, Your Honor."

"You have not given the defendant the benefit of any doubt whatsoever, Miss Evans. The articles that have appeared in the *Times* I would characterize as little short of virulent."

"Your Honor, I have merely done my duty."

"So I am to understand. I meant merely that it is a matter of public record that Mr. Fabry's literary efforts are regularly excoriated in your columns —"

"Objection, Your Honor," exclaimed Marianne's solicitor. "We are here to decide upon the evidence, not to discuss the merits of my client's literary tastes."

"Quite true," the judge admitted. "Let us now hear from the experts."

A kind of shudder rippled through the audience. The case was entering the decisive phase. Sitting in the back of the room, I began to tremble at the thought that I had left out some detail in my work, that it would be seen through as a fraud. Everything now hinged upon two men dressed like morticians. I closed my eyes to listen to their opinion, like a patient waiting for the doctor to read the lab reports on a tumor.

In language that was insufferably technical and unnecessarily precise, each gentleman in turn reviewed the history of printing beginning with Gutenberg. I was in agony waiting for them to come to their conclusions. Happily, the audience, which had begun by hanging on their every word, started to grumble and whisper, and though the spectators were summarily hushed by the judge, the experts got the point. They began to talk about the book.

I held my breath, but it wasn't long before I could breathe normally. The paper, the ink, the glues, the thread, and the casing were perfectly authentic. Without any shadow of a reasonable doubt, they said, *The Need to Love* was a period piece. The experts concluded that the book had most likely been printed before World War II, or at the very latest sometime during the 1940s. The date printed in the work, 1939, was the most plausible.

The room erupted. The judge pounded his gavel and demanded silence, but for a few minutes it was to no avail. I had created a most satisfactory scandal.

When order was restored, Nicolas's solicitor rose to say that they would seek a second opinion. The request was granted. The judge asked that the forensic laboratory at Scotland Yard be accorded the task. Until then, there would be no decision as to how to rule on Nicolas's suit. The delay didn't worry me. I was confident that my work would prove infallible and that Scotland Yard's best would arrive at the same conclusion.

I didn't have the courage to find Nicolas and comfort him, though I knew it must have been a genuinely horrible experience for him. Instead, like a coward, I escaped to my office.

A package was waiting for me on my desk. It was a copy of *The Need to Love* that a bookseller had sent on from Southampton. Several days earlier I had issued a search request to every secondhand bookshop in England, at Millagard's urging, to locate other extant copies of my masterpiece. My message-bearing bottles were coming home.

I rang up Millagard at his hotel to tell him of my "discovery."

I heard him sigh.

"That isn't going to help our case."

"On the contrary," I replied. "Who's to say if this copy is identical to Miss Evans's? Think about it, Laurent. If I give this copy to the forensic laboratory at Scotland Yard, isn't there the possibility they'll detect a difference?"

"And if they don't? It would be doubly damning."

"Quite so," I agreed. "But we won't lose anything by trying."

"All right, Edward. I give you carte blanche."

I asked how Nicolas was holding up, for the cruel pleasure of hearing that he wasn't.

"I'm beginning to think he's going off the deep end," Millagard confided. "He's ranting about how he is going to flay Marianne Evans alive."

"Good heavens. Try to keep him from doing anything foolish. And don't lose hope, old man, for God's sake. In two weeks we'll be through all this."

I rang off and went home to put the final touch on my plan. From my safe, I took the medical file I'd made off with when Nicolas was in hospital. I found an ordinary unmarked envelope and addressed it to *People* magazine, then slipped the file inside. If the second found copy of *The Need to Love* was going to fuel the controversy, this little document would definitively weigh the scales on the side of imminent justice.

I slept fitfully the next few nights. Partly this was because of the remorse I felt creeping over me at moments for betraying Nicolas. However, even more, it was from a growing fear that I might betray myself. It began as a vague suspicion at first, but it soon turned into a full-blown obsession. I fretted that one day I would admit to what I had done, compelled by the same masochistic pride that drives some criminals to boast about crimes for which they were never caught. Might I do this, I wondered? How could I be sure? Unless you possess the thick skin of a seasoned professional killer, there is no way of knowing, and no way of stopping this fear. I learned to live with it.

Each morning I woke up exhausted but grimly determined not to stop the machine I had set into motion. Upsetting as this whole episode was, I would see it through. No longer was it a question of revenge; it was a question of justice. Besides, were I to stay my hand from pity, the consequences for me would be truly terrible.

I had great respect for the power of my hatred, and this gave me courage. It carried me. I wondered if I would fall apart when the hate was gone.

The three weeks preceding the second hearing dragged on. I spent much of them pacing around my office in circles, virtually incapable of concentrating on my work. Each week I read through *People,* looking for a story on Nicolas's medical history, but there was nothing. My guess was that they were holding off until the eve of the second hearing, when public interest would be at its peak.

I went out walking only once, out of an urgent need to get some air, and took advantage of the occasion to resolve the issue of rights to C. Irving Brown's book. I called upon Anthony Ramsay, Philip Ramsay's nephew, having already telephoned and explained why I wanted to meet with him. He confirmed that he was the only living relative of his uncle and said he would be willing to discuss the matter. At the appointed hour we met, and he presented me with Philip Ramsay's last will and testament, dating from 1940, naming him as heir. I explained my somewhat paradoxical position. Being the English publisher of Nicolas Fabry, I wanted to acquire the rights for C. Irving Brown's novel from Marble Arch Press, which had published *The Need to Love* in 1939. I explained I was willing to do this before hearing the latest test results, which could, after all, prove the whole thing a fraud. The countersuit claims would be my responsibility if he accepted my preemptive offer. Turner Press would undertake all obligations as pertains any future heirs of C. Irving Brown.

My honesty seemed to have pleased the man, who had never thought he would get a penny from Marble Arch. At the time of his uncle's death, the press had had only three or four titles in circulation. What's more, he made no attempt to push the price higher than the five thousand pounds I offered, though I would of course have gone higher — considerably higher. Without hesitating, he signed the agreement I had brought with me. I wrote him out a check.

Thoroughly delighted with myself, I walked back to my office, taking in the sights at a leisurely pace, something I hadn't done since my visit to Vichy.

"Sir Edward, just what is the point of this agreement?" my solicitor Vanderon asked me when, several days later, I presented him with the contract.

"Very simple, really. Imagine that Brown does

have heirs. If plagiarism is established as fact, Laurent Millagard would be forced to transfer to her or him whatever rights Nicolas had to *Il faut aimer*. That will inevitably mean another trial. I don't doubt but that Millagard will be ruined. Now imagine he doesn't have any heirs. By acquiring all rights from Marble Arch Press, I have an advantage over Millagard and Fabry, since not only am I free to reissue *The Need to Love*, I get what would have gone to the author or his heirs."

Though not expressive by nature, Vanderon was unable to repress an appreciative smile. "You should have read law, Sir Edward," he said, in a voice that nearly expressed admiration.

Chapter 12

As I had suspected, the day before the second hearing *People* printed Nicolas's medical file in a grand story on the very first page. Its reporters pretended that they had discovered this exciting bit of evidence on their own. I was only too happy to let them have the credit.

The article quoted at length a well-known psychiatrist who explained that the "Fabrycation Affair" was far from being a simple case of plagiarism. Rather, it was a case of "cryptoamnesia," as he called it. What this meant was that Nicolas could have read *The Need to Love,* and that his occasional amnesia had permitted him to be unconscious that he had done so, yet at the same time retaining each and every word in his subconscious.

The piece amused me greatly. That night I slept soundly.

The second opinion sought by the solicitors merely confirmed authenticity. *The Need to Love* was no forgery. Having analyzed several works published by Marble Arch Press, the Scotland Yard experts determined that the correspondences between *The Need to Love* and what remained of the Marble Arch Press's books were clear in all the elements of design and production.

Undaunted, Nicolas launched into his self-defense. Brandishing a typescript covered with corrections and yellow tags, he professed his innocence. In an attempt to salvage his reputation, he turned himself into a pitiful spectacle and talked openly about his fears about never becoming a truly great writer, about how he had been a prisoner of his own authorial indifference, and about how in *Il faut aimer* he had revealed his true self to the world as never before in his work, to "achieve the most complete form of sincerity" of which his masterpiece was the highest proof.

The judge listened to him with the smile of skepticism. Marianne Evans adjusted her hair and struck fetching poses.

This was too much for Nicolas. He started to shout, gesticulate wildly, shake his fist at the court, and generally accuse English justice of the same perfidy with which it had condemned Joan of Arc.

"There is something rotten in the Kingdom of England!" he thundered.

This was greeted with a chorus of indignation. The judge restored order, then solemnly opened a thin folder and read it over for a few moments before breaking the heavy silence that hung over the room.

"Mr. Fabry," he began, "you see fit to accuse the

United Kingdom of plotting against you and your countrymen. Happily, your military career suggests how insincere the accusation, given that you are in an excellent position to know that the British people came to the rescue of your country during the last war. Were it not for your past heroism during that great conflict I would hold you in contempt of this court."

"Your Honor!" interrupted Nicolas's solicitor. "We are not here to judge anyone's military record, in particular my client's — which, as you suggest, is a distinguished one. Rather, we here are to consider the accusation brought against him by Miss Ev —"

"I quite agree," the judge broke in, "and I was only making reference to your client's distinguished record in response to his typically French accusation that — In any event, since that subject has been raised, I believe there is a new element to introduce, an element that was not known at the time of the first hearing. I am referring to the leakage to the print media of Mr. Fabry's military file, and the fact that it offers an alternative to the possibility of plagiarism on his part."

A murmur of surprise rippled through the gallery. Nicolas sat up straight in his chair.

"I am specifically referring to what happened to Captain Fabry on July 17, 1943, when, during the course of a mission, he fell victim to an accident that left him — if I am to believe this report — with rather serious cerebral repercussions."

"This is an outrage!" shouted Nicolas. "I was a

hero! I was awarded the O.B.E., made a member of the Legion of Honor. I am completely fit in mind and body!"

"I wish I believed it so," said the judge, sighing. "Nonetheless, the document I am holding is entirely authentic."

He waved the paper he had removed from the folder in the air.

"I have never been aware of such a document," cried Nicolas. "You cannot admit it for use in this hearing!"

"Your objection notwithstanding," continued the judge, "this medical report would explain in an entirely logical fashion your having — how shall I put it? — 'unconsciously borrowed' from Mr. Brown's opus, even if the material proof had not already established that very fact."

I am at a loss to describe the emotions that swirled around the room. All I heard was the beating of my heart, and I felt a mixture of triumph and nausea. My victory had left me with no strength. I do believe that at that instant I felt true pity for Nicolas. But I would not even then have given way to that cowardly compassion that even tyrants can inspire at the moment of their demise.

There was a brief recess, after which the judge rendered his verdict: the court rejected Nicolas Fabry's countersuit and ordered the plaintiff to cover all costs.

In the havoc that followed I spotted Marianne Evans making her way through the crowd, looking arrogantly serene. The bitch! Then I saw Nicolas — again — facing a barrage of cameras and flashes on the steps of the Old Bailey, defeated but defiant. I felt a jealous pang at the strength he still managed to summon to proclaim his innocence. I admired the theatrical gesture of throwing his manuscript into the air. Damn the man! He could still find a way of being handsome, dashing, and — despite it all — graceful. Under the same circumstances all I would have managed to do was vomit. In his place I would have looked small and gray and shabby.

Not Nicolas. He kept his air of dismissive defiance when he announced that now the legalities were over and he had no choice but to accept this decision, he would remain in England until he had tracked down this so-called C. Irving Brown, whose work absolutely no one seemed to remember — "How very convenient!"

His innocence fairly cried out. I was relieved that Doris wasn't there. She is very sensitive. Doubtless she would have turned to me with a questioning look.

"My reputation may be ruined," continued Nicolas in a clear and steady voice, "but I will prove to all of you that I am an authentic writer, that my gifts are mine and mine alone."

I managed to get him to climb into my car and drove him and Millagard to the Savoy. I had reserved him the best suite available, proof that my opinion of him hadn't changed. I also felt I owed it to him. Millagard, knowing that difficult financial times were ahead, had selected a less expensive accomodation.

Nicolas never stopped talking — about the judge, Marianne Evans, England.

"All that anyone has found to give this C. Irving

Brown reality, and to destroy my life, is two miserable dog-eared volumes. Diabolical! Do you really think that for one second I believe in the existence of this phantom? Until someone proves otherwise, I am the only, the sole, and the glorious author of *Il faut aimer*, my masterpiece. ME."

I kept my thoughts to myself. I was waiting for him to utter Yasmina's name. Why could he not see that what had happened contained some element of justice, that any literary prize based upon a crime, a deep and grievous wrong, could only bring misery? I was waiting for him to admit to what he had done to me and to Yasmina. It wasn't just him. Why didn't he see all this? Why did only I see it?

Nicolas carried on his monologue from the backseat, sliding from one side to the other like a trapped rat seeking a way out. Millagard and I stared silently straight ahead.

"I want to see another one!" Nicolas cried suddenly. "Another copy of this book! Do you understand? I want to see it, touch it, feel it. I'm going through every public library in England with a fine-toothed comb!"

"No need to go running around to libraries," I said. "Every specialty bookshop in the country has been alerted to inform me immediately should they locate another copy of *The Need to Love*."

"Not enough!" he bellowed in my ear. "I want to learn everything I can about this man! Everything!"

"Very well," I replied. "Since you seem so intent on it, since you want to pour salt in the wound, we'll start our search tomorrow. I'll contact an old army friend of mine from the Dorchester days. There's a chance he might let us have a look at Brown's military file."

I dropped them off at the hotel. We had settled on a time to meet the following day at my office. From there we would go down to Ipswich, Brown's hometown, then to the War Office. Millagard thanked me warmly for all my efforts. Nicolas, who expected such devotion, said nothing.

Driving home, a chill went down my spine. What on earth had possessed me to promise Nicolas and Millagard I would contact my Dorchester friend about a military file? It seemed certain to set anyone beginning to have suspicions about me to thinking. Given his present state of mind, Nicolas wouldn't guess the part I was playing in his downfall, probably not even suspect that someone might have obtained his military record through precisely the same means. Millagard, on the other hand, might. For all his panic, he had a subtle mind. How would he interpret my offer? In his place, it seemed to me I would have sniffed a plot — would have begun to see that Sir Edward Destry was indeed the only person in the world with all the necessary elements to concoct the whole bloody thing. It all added up: I had been a forger during the war and a printer; I was a publisher; I was an expert in contemporary British literature; I was the English translator of Nicolas's previous novels. And I had every reason to be jealous. You didn't need to be Sherlock Holmes to suspect I might be involved.

On the other hand, I reasoned, forcing back the fear, how could anyone believe that a publisher would be crazy enough to destroy the career of one of his most successful writers and oldest friends?

I would need to be very careful with myself. By telling them I could get access to Brown's file, I was showing distinct signs of an impulse to confess. That would explain why I was making allusions of a more or less subtle nature, and playing with puns and hints. Now that the verdict had been rendered, the only thing of interest left for me was whether or not I would spill the beans. The game had started to lose interest. It galled me that having to keep my triumph a secret deprived me of the most stunning victory I had ever known.

I also suspected that I was softening. My opinion of Nicolas had begun to change. Pitiful was all he really was. Listening to him rant and rave in the car on the way to the hotel, I had nearly wanted to laugh, as children laugh at someone with a disability. It was another sign that I was distancing myself from my plot.

Instead of returning to my apartment, I went by the Turner Press offices. As if reflecting my own feelings, the staff was depressed. Doris looked as if she were struggling to hold back tears, and indeed the minute she saw me she burst into sobs. The rest stared vacantly at the work on their desks.

My firm intention was to get back to work and put the whole dreadful business behind me. I had been ignoring the company's business for months; mail had been piling up; my shelves were covered with unread manuscripts; there were piles of contracts I needed to review, payments to approve, invoices to consider. I had no heart for it. I was swept up in a conviction of the worthlessness of it all. What had I really accomplished? Ruined the career of a gifted writer, that's what. The feeling of liberation that I had expected had not come. The wellspring of my genius, which Nicolas had kept captive, was not mine after all. The whole thing had been an exercise in self-deception.

I opened the bottom drawer of my desk. The barrel of my revolver was visible. One bullet would be enough. I picked up the gun and cradled its heft in the palm of my hand.

At that moment my intercom buzzed. I put the revolver back in the drawer.

"Yes, what is it?" I asked in a thick voice.

"Sir Edward, if it's all right with you I'd like to leave now," replied Doris, "Unless you need me for anything."

"No, Doris. Please do go ahead. It's just past six, and I'll soon be leaving as well. It has been a difficult day. Good night, Doris."

The moment of self-destructiveness had passed, but I must have stayed another two hours in my office, wallowing in self-pity, feeling as if I was already among the dead. All that remained of life was to bear, until the end of my miserable days, the terrible burden of guilt for what I had done —

What about Nicolas? What would he do? What would happen when he found the copy of *The Need to*

Love that I had placed in his study? He would have no further doubt of his guilt — involuntary guilt though it might be. To sin from amnesia is no sin, though the whole idea would throw into doubt the creative process. With every line he wrote, the man would wonder whether he wasn't just copying out someone else's book. And if Nicolas never found that third copy? He would be condemned, as I was, to live with the agony of uncertainty.

A miserable way to survive.

Chapter 13

The following morning, as I had promised, I drove Nicolas and Millagard to Ipswich. A fine, icy rain was falling. We prowled up and down Dickens Road and studied the houses — which looked appropriately Victorian, with their grimy red brick and tiny gardens — for more than an hour.

A despondent Nicolas carefully examined the former abode of C. Irving Brown, perhaps with the hope of finding somewhere among its gloomy gables the key to the mystery that had ravaged his life. He must have wondered how his double could have inhabited such a lugubrious place and still write a book that in its glorious descriptions of Egyptian splendors was the twin to his own.

"Only one person can solve this mystery," he concluded finally. "That witch Marianne Evans! The idea of meeting with her revolts me, but I must know if she has done this thing to me. How can anyone's hate be that strong?"

These last words made me tremble. What if Marianne Evans, moved by Nicolas's entreaties, admitted that Brown's book had come to her anonymously? What if she were suddenly to become interested in the person who sent it?

Nicolas would devote his life to looking for the wretched creature.

I gathered together all my persuasive powers to dissuade him from seeking a meeting with Evans, which could, I assured him, have disastrous consequences. Evans might accuse him of threatening her with physical violence. Luckily, Millagard agreed with me. To distract them from further discussion of the idea, I drove them to the Defense Ministry, where my friend had Brown's military file waiting for us.

As I had known, the slim green folder contained nothing of use. Inside were three typed forms and an identity photo. The photo made Brown look even more like a ghost — downcast eyes, haggard expression. He looked as if he were embarrassed to be seen. As to his record, there was nothing extraordinary about it. He had died a banal death under the strafing fire of Goering's Stuka dive-bombers.

I saw that Nicolas was deeply disappointed at how little Brown's record and his own had in common. He might have accepted his fate better had Brown at least flattered his narcissism.

We had to struggle again to keep Nicolas from going to see "that bitch Evans." Finally, exasperated, Millagard announced that he would be finished with this madman if he didn't join him on the next flight back to Paris.

"You are all abandoning me!" Nicolas cried. "You whose coffers I have been filling for twenty years! You bastards! You filthy fucking bastards!"

But Millagard really had had it and wouldn't retreat. Calling Nicolas insane and self-centered, he shoved him against the backseat of the car. I had never seen this timid publisher so incensed as to attack one of his own authors.

I drove them to Heathrow. The rain came down in sheets. Millagard and I talked.

"This business is not finished," he said grimly. "I have thought long and hard about it. There is still another danger. If by some miserable chance this C. Irving Brown has an heir, I may as well hand over to him the keys to the publishing house."

"What do you mean?" I asked, trying to look surprised.

"I mean that if there is an heir I will have not only to turn over all profits earned on the sale of more than 300,000 copies of *Il faut aimer* but also reimburse him for compensatory damages for having published an unauthorized 'adaptation.'"

"Ah."

"The solution is for you to purchase the estate of Marble Arch Press, thereby making yourself legal heir and inheriting the proceeds a publisher owes an author."

"But Brown doesn't seem to have any heirs."

"Two precautions are better than one. If it comes to it, you could threaten to sue me, that would allow me to transfer to you those rights which would have belonged to Brown. Do you follow me?"

I managed to look as if I found what he was telling me admirably clear. What was most important for Millagard was to avoid the financial risk involved in being sued for forgery. The London court had not settled this issue, contenting itself with authenticating *The Need to Love* and denying Nicolas's countersuit for defamation. Still, I felt a sudden doubt. Could this be a trap? Had Millagard learned that I'd already negotiated for the estate of Marble Arch Press with Philip Ramsay's nephew? I dismissed the idea. He looked far too sincere to be playing that cool a game.

At this point in the conversation, Nicolas leaned forward.

"I'm going away," he bawled. "I'm going away. Far away!"

We pretended not to hear him.

I left Nicolas and Millagard at the airport and drove back to London. I was going back to work, seriously this time, and would wait for the moment when Nicolas found his copy of the book. That should finish it. I knew Nicolas well enough to know that finding it would be too much for him.

To live with expectation is to live in hope and fear, torment and joy, and I was no exception to this rule. Nicolas was a courageous man. If he got through this dark period of his life it was entirely possible he would write yet another novel, perhaps one as brilliant as the last. That thought gave me chills. Images of him confronted me everywhere — in the street, in my office, in my dreams. I imagined Nicolas covered with glory once again, me crushed as before beneath the weight of his superiority, blinded by his name emblazoned on the jacket of a book.

Why would he not just confess to his amnesia, after all? Simply admit his unconscious error to the public, and by so doing attract their sympathy and understanding? He was, after all, only a victim of his own wartime heroism. No shame in that.

Perhaps he would conceive of writing about his "cryptoamnesia," and with great subtlety and insight, thereby capitalizing on his accident and its consequences. The act of writing about it would free him of opprobrium.

I could just see him holed up in his study, the blinds closed, hard at work on this new masterpiece. Time was on his side. Once more he would find a way of depriving me of life.

My moods changed. These were my worst fears. There were other moments when I managed to enjoy what I had accomplished. And I suspected that despite it all my life would roll along as smoothly as a Bentley. I would find new writers, publish new books, create new profits. My new fears were the shadows of older fears. During the moments of euphoria, I felt a very strong temptation to confess everything to Doris.

One day a letter from Nicolas arrived on my desk.

"I've made up my mind," it began. "I'm going to Brazil. To Manaus. The jungle's profusion will conceal me from the demons that haunt me. Start from scratch. No other way. I have hit bottom, but I am free. I can begin again, be reborn. Good-bye."

I made a few pitiful attempts to keep him from

leaving. I wanted him to stay in Paris, to look through his books, and to find the copy of *The Need to Love* that I had intended for him. I talked to Millagard and said he should urge Nicolas to stay, to face up to his detractors. He replied he had no intention to coddle Nicolas until the end of his days, and that as far as he was concerned going to Brazil was a fine idea.

I called Peter at his school in Gstaad to ask him to talk to his father. Peter replied that he didn't want anything to do with "this whole crazy business," and that anyway, his father always did as he pleased. I was ashamed of myself for having tried to use Peter, whom I loved, and I didn't push the matter further.

The bitter tone in Peter's voice wounded me. Up to then I had thought him untouched by the scandal, given that he had so little contact with his father and was so far from him physically. To learn that he had gotten into a fight with his best friend, a French boy, because the latter had called him "Little Boy Brown" was truly painful.

So I conceded defeat and resigned myself to the fact that eventually a letter would come informing me of Nicolas's miraculous "resurrection."

In his first letter from Brazil he wrote that with all its seductions and sirens, the New World had cured him of the urge to write. The writing life that he had led for so long, seen from afar, seemed ridiculous.

"I have become absorbed by an exquisite sensuality in which the only ink is the sap of trees and bodies."

The next letter was more explicit.

"Eulelia's body, lying next to me, glistens like

gold and gives off blinding power. Her pidgin French, a relic of a church school, enchants me. The varieties and vagaries of her fantasies are limitless and extraordinary. She conceals her professionalism beneath naive charm."

Some months later, yet another letter announced he was coming back.

> There is nothing more for me here. I probably should have adapted to the idea of expiating my sins through exile, but I actually continue to believe in my innocence. One might accept being a thief or a murderer. But not someone possessed by an invisible devil. I cannot spend my life running away to the ends of the earth. I refuse to act the part of the pariah, the one you might hear about on some street: "Fabry? You mean the famous plagiarist? I'd heard he'd gone native somewhere in the Amazonian Basin."
>
> Now that I have recovered somewhat, I will come home and face things squarely. I am no grave-robber. I do not steal manuscripts from the dead, like Sholokhov did with the first volume of *Quiet Flows the Don* (at least according to Solzhenitsyn). Have I not written a body of work that proves my abilities? The accusation of plagiarism is naive and simplistic, and leaves me feeling more indifferent than ever.

If Nicolas were going to prove game enough to come home, I would have to be the one to leave. My affairs were in order and had been for some time. In my will I left a good deal of Turner Press to the staff, reserving the major portion for Peter, who I knew had become passionately interested in literature. He would also get my flat in Chelsea. Everything else would go to various charitable organizations. And as for my own personal copy of *The Need to Love,* Marianne Evans was the only logical recipient. I also planned to give her the proofs and original manuscript, and had written a letter explaining everything.

"When you read these lines," it began,

> I will have returned to dust. But from the bottom of my living heart I thank you for contributing so much to the cleverest literary scam our drab century has produced. I suspect you will take this news with you to the grave, and remain my only judge, but I thought you should know you played your role magnificently, and hope you do not resent me for having chosen you for the part. You see, I knew your need for revenge was nearly as powerful as my own. Please accept this small token of thanks.

This letter, a finished copy of *The Need to Love* together with galleys, and my will were all sealed in an envelope at the bottom of the safe in my country house. There would be time to give it to John Holland in due course.

I tried several times to call Paris, to learn whether Nicolas was back, but no one answered. A month passed. Finally, one day, a call came from Heathrow. It was from an Air France pilot who said he was an old friend of Nicolas. Nicolas had given him an envelope two hours earlier and asked that it be put directly into my hands.

I hurried out to the airport. Sitting in my car in the parking lot, I opened the envelope, pulled out a small pile of papers, and immediately set to reading them.

You may have tried to call me. I disconnected the phone. No one else besides Nora knows that I am back from Brazil. It has been two months since I've been going in circles, circling the abyss, spinning together memories, questions, anxieties. Writing my last book put me through so much soul-searching. I knew that up to that point my work had tasted of usury and of death. I'd become as hollow as an old stump. All I'd really done was satiate my fantasies and apply them to different literary styles. Until I thought of writing about the story of Farida, Yasmina, that Egyptian girl I'd gotten pregnant so many years ago and who then killed herself. Because of me. I never spoke to you about it. It was my secret. The words seemed to come spilling out on the page, and the novel rose through me like a spasm of pleasure. Everything was new again.

Nora came to my house eight days ago. She managed to sneak by the concierge, despite my orders to admit no one. She moved back in. Her looks of sympathy I found revolting. It was the Egyptian dancing girl I had always loved in her. Now she was nothing but a nurse. I don't know. Perhaps she had to come back for my destiny to be fulfilled.

What possessed her to decide to organize my books? To distract me from my agonies?

You know that I have never thrown out a single book or given one away. If I lose one, I have to buy another copy of it. I must have 6,000 books by now, and for many of them I couldn't give you title or author.

We started by putting them into alphabetical order according to author. A slow process. I will admit I started to enjoy it, for it distracted from darker thoughts. Then Nora found a little blue book on whose damaged spine a name was printed with gold lettering: C. Irving Brown.

Cold horror. I was pushed into the darkness of a bottomless crevasse of ice.

Like the other two copies, it has no dust jacket. The cover was slightly singed, as are some of the pages. But on the whole it survived in good shape. A price is written in pencil on the flyleaf, the way they do in old books of interest only to collectors. Two shillings.

I have been reading and rereading it over and over. It is truly staggering. How could my novel, page after page of my own work, resemble Brown's novel in so many details? How is it possible that I could have retained in the unconscious folds of my memory so much of his text? How, without knowing it, could I have captured in nearly photographic fashion Brown's book, before burying it thirty-years-deep in the secret labyrinths of my mind? How? Because the story was so similar to something I had lived? Because it was about a tragic affair with a young girl who in every respect was Yasmina's double? But they were mine, those nights of love! They were ours! Our midnight walks along the shore, that crazy evening on Pharos — I was the one who lived them with her! They were mine! At least, they were before the accident. Could it have been that this English cipher had dreamed precisely the same things I had actually lived? Had fantasized exactly the same feelings I had actually experienced? That way, madness.

When I read this novel thirty years ago, I must have been fascinated by the similarities and devoured it without dropping so much as a single word, too swept away even to scrawl something in the margins the way I normally do. This absence of marginalia makes me think that, after all, I am "guilty."

One thing is certain. I will never write again. How could I ever be sure that I was the author of my ideas and my expressions? Is that metaphor mine? What about that imagery? Did I make up that character? How can I be sure? Writing was the one thing upon which I counted to tell me I was unique and that I was alive.

When all is said and done, you know, the scandal surrounding *Il faut aimer* is a magnificent amalgam of glory and humiliation, and it remains the "highwire act of genius" that some critics called it when it first appeared. That is what I think, and I really don't care what history decides. Probably in the future my name will be inexorably linked to a clinical case of interest only to students of psychiatry. The "Fabry Phenomenon" will be my claim to immortal fame. I really don't care.

Time to cross the bar. I am sorry not to see Peter grow up. I am sorry, too, for all the women who I could not bring myself to love. None of them are worth staying for.

If I had one wish, it would be that someday someone would write of me as the true father of *Il faut aimer*. Because, you see, bastard though it be, I think it my finest offspring.

Nicolas

I ran to the nearest telephone and called Millagard. He confirmed what the letter had said. Nora had found Nicolas's body at 9:13 P.M. on the floor of his study, a bullet through the brain.

Chapter 14

There was quite a crowd at the cemetery. All the women that Nicolas had never been able to bring himself to love had come to say farewell. Anne, remarried and living in Canada, had decided not to attend. Flu prevented Peter from leaving Gstaad, which was a very good thing, I thought. There were lots of official-looking people from the Compagnons de la Libération and plenty of people from the publishing world. But mostly there were women. The overpowering smell of perfume was proof enough that the man we were burying had not lived a chaste life.

Given the manner of Nicolas's death, no grand eulogies were given. A priest said a few simple words about fame, courage, despair, and Divine Mercy, and offered prayers to the heavens. For my part, I threw a handful of dirt on the coffin. A grief-stricken Millagard saw my half-smile and gave me a puzzled look.

Nora hid her tears behind a black veil and held on to my hand for a long time.

"You were his best friend," she told me. "He loved you very much and spoke often of your growing up together in Alexandria."

This caused me pain. I wanted to get away from everyone as quickly as possible, but Millagard insisted on driving me to the airport, and I could hardly refuse the offer.

We sat in silence for a while. I heard him sniffle and realized that he was truly saddened by Nicolas's death.

Suddenly, to my alarm, he burst into sobs, like a child.

"Damn it all! I loved him, Edward. I loved him. . . . Despite everything that he did to me, I loved him. What a man he was — magnificent, funny, moving." Millagard wiped his eyes. "You know, if we hadn't had formal proof of his amnesia I never would have bought that plagiarism story. And you know why? Because that just was not something he would do, that's why. He was the real thing. I still don't buy it completely. It just doesn't add up somehow, but I'll be damned if I can put my finger on why."

The trip was an insufferable one for me, but thank the good Lord it didn't last long, and with enormous relief I managed to detach myself from Millagard.

I spent the next two days in a state of near-total disorientation. It was a very good thing I had so much work to do. Happily, too, all the agitation caused by Nicolas's death quickly passed. His suicide was widely regarded as an admission of guilt, and after a few days the tabloids and gossipmongers had moved on to other, fresher scandals. Only the lawyers didn't lose interest in the case. The problem of copyright ownership for *Il faut aimer* was not fully resolved.

I permitted myself the luxury of magnanimity. Having repurchased all rights to Marble Arch Press titles, I had in effect replaced Brown's legal heirs in terms of claiming the profits earned in France on Nicolas's last book. I needed to bring the suit against Millagard formally, given that the English court had gone no further than verifying the authenticity of *The Need to Love* and rejecting the basis for Nicolas's countersuit. Sir Charles Vanderon urged me to push ahead, but I refused. Justice had been served. I decided to allow Nicolas to remain the beneficiary of any "legal" doubt in the matter.

The only causes I wanted to advance were those of sparing my loyal colleague in France further anguish and allowing Peter to profit from the royalties of his father's book, which had outsold all his previous books. I was content with world rights to Brown's book — which, naturally, I was planning to reissue in paperback.

The Need to Love, would, I was sure, enjoy such tremendous commercial success that I would be able to afford my generosity. Millagard, of course, was thrilled with the arrangement. Not so Peter, who was furious at the idea I was reissuing the original, complete with a biographical sketch of Brown and a brief introduction in which I explained that I felt honorbound as a publisher to offer to the public the right to judge for themselves the "celebrated and troubling similarities" between the two texts. The final verdict lay in the hearts and minds of readers.

Peter defended his father vehemently, something he had never done when Nicolas was alive. He called me all sorts of names. I decided that his response was emotional and that he was still getting at his father through me. In time he would see this and understand, as Millagard did, that I had handled things fairly.

For me, the passage of time changed almost nothing. The Death of the Author had not restored to me any creativity. I tried, unsuccessfully, to write.

Did my lack of creative talent have nothing to do with Nicolas Fabry?

Two weeks after *The Need to Love* appeared, a call came for me from Burgleyhad, in Scotland.

"I am so sorry to disturb you," a voice told me in a pleasant, slightly lilting voice. "My name is Ossiana Macpherson. A friend gave me a copy of *The Need to Love* and I haven't been able to put it down! You see, I had no idea that my brother had published a novel."

"I beg your pardon?"

"Yes. I'm C. Irving Brown's sister."

The sky had come crashing down upon my head. Sweat poured out. I felt as if I were watching the collapse of my magnificent creation. I started babbling shamefully, then attempted to collect my thoughts.

"Mrs. Macpherson, you must think me a dithering idiot. It's just that I'm rather taken aback, you see! Do you think you could come round to my office? Right away, if it's not too inconvenient?"

"I'm afraid that I can't leave Burgleyhad."

She explained that since the death of her husband,

she was alone in raising greyhounds in a remote corner of the country, and positively could not leave home for more than a few hours at most. I therefore proposed going up to see her in Burgleyhad, a proposition she accepted with enthusiasm. I told her I would be arriving the next day.

Very early the next morning I took a train to Inverness, where I hired a car to cover the remaining forty-five miles. I thought I would never arrive. I was awash in new sensations, just when I thought I had exhausted the whole register of human emotions these last few months. My skin felt prickly, my arms stiff, and I was having difficulty breathing.

Finally, I was there — 21 Stuart Lane, Burgleyhad, a modest, clean little town that couldn't have held more than a few hundred inhabitants. Seeing it helped me understand why Brown's sister had not heard anything about the whole Fabry business.

She lived in a small house, much like the ones you find in illustrated children's books on Scotland. The roof was thatched. Vines and roses clung to the whitewashed walls. The front wall was covered with moss. At the back of a garden filled with flowers was a partly covered enclosure, which I assumed served as a kennel.

I didn't have to ring the bell. A woman, in her fifties I guessed, and still very attractive, opened the door. She seemed very fit, with the rosy, glowing complexion that comes with healthy living. Her hair was long and free-flowing. We introduced ourselves, and I followed her into the house. The sitting room was cozy and comfortable and showed perfect taste. Here and there were bits of exotica. She inquired politely how my trip had gone and apologized for all the trouble I had gone to to reach her. I found her smile charming, and her blue-eyed expression seemed honest and open. Yet I was very much on my guard. This woman could, after all, bring about my downfall.

I had sat down in an overstuffed chair with a flowery pattern, and she came directly to the point.

"I thought I should repeat what I told you on the phone yesterday. I don't understand this whole business about my brother and this novel."

"Nonetheless, madam, it is true. It was published by Marble Arch Press, whose rights I have purchased."

"Yes, I understand all that. I did read your introduction. But Chatterton could not have written it."

"How can you be so sure?"

"Well, I am his sister, after all. I should know, don't you think?"

I crossed my legs and took a deep breath.

"Mrs. Macpherson, permit me to try and explain what I believe occurred. Due to the bombing during the Blitz, the novel was never properly distributed. All that remained of the printing were some half-dozen copies. Your brother probably died without knowing the book had even been published."

"Fine. Imagine that I accept this as true. After all, I was a girl at the time, and Chatterton was a few years older. The only thing I was interested in then was horses. But what about our parents?"

"Ah, yes. Well, you see, parents are a little like cuckolded spouses, aren't they? Always the last to know."

Not very elegant, I will admit. But I doggedly

pressed onward with the idea that young writers very often submit their manuscript in secrecy, without having told a living soul they've written it. Frequently this is because their parents would be aghast that their children are thinking of becoming writers, when they ought to become bankers, lawyers, and accountants. Writing for a living is a very unwise thing to do.

I could see I was bringing her round. All she really wanted was to be convinced; because the royalties that would come to her would be very handsome. For a widow raising dogs in a remote corner of Scotland, the money was a godsend.

She showed me some photos of her brother. There he was at last, my author, in the flesh. I was thrilled. His handwriting appeared on some of them, and I noted that it was slanted and precise. Very much like mine. So too his background — a studious teenager with a ravenous appetite for books and for secrecy, and hampered by tremendous shyness. It was him. I knew it.

The time seemed to fly. I could have spent many happy hours talking with Ossiana Macpherson, and I asked if she would join me for dinner at the finest restaurant in the village. She accepted with a dazzling smile.

We went to a charming little country inn. She let me choose the menu and was delighted when I ordered a bottle of Bordeaux, the best claret on the list. As a rule I am very awkward on first dates, but this was a euphoric exception.

There are moments in life when we have everything we desire, when we are simply and completely happy. The peace I felt with Ossiana cleansed my sins and justified my crimes. We talked as if we had known each other for ages. She was fascinated by everything I had to say, wishing to know all about my life, my profession, my experiences in the war. She remarked on the color of my eyes, my only remarkable feature. For my part, I was swept up by the tenderest of feelings for her. Putting my hand on hers, I told her with a deep sigh that it seemed like ages since we hadn't known each other.

She smiled and let her hand remain beneath mine. What pure joy that smile was to me.

After the coffee, she suddenly gave a start.

"I just remembered something! If you're not in too great a rush, we could make a quick trip up to my attic. That's where I keep Chatterton's old trunk. I've never been through it carefully, but I remember it was filled with his papers."

We returned to her house. I was filled with apprehension. Would there be something in that trunk that would bring down my house of cards? A diary, perhaps? Anything that might make it clear that C. Irving could not have written a novel?

Ossiana jumped out of the car as nimbly as a young girl. With me huffing behind, she shinnied up the ladder to the attic. My heart was pounding. Beneath piles of boxes and behind dusty furniture, she found the trunk in question.

"Here it is. I don't believe it's been touched since I moved from Ipswich. How funny! I can't imagine what we'll find."

I undid the latches and raised the lid, slowly, like

someone opening a casket. Inside were books, clippings, notebooks, lecture notes, letters. At the bottom lay a black moleskin folder, which I immediately opened and began looking through, a cold sweat beading my forehead. Three hundred pages of writing. It was not a diary. It was a manuscript. On the title page was handwritten in large letters: *Only the Journey Matters: A Novel by C. Irving Brown*.

My cry of relief was also an exclamation of joy. Ossiana saw what it was and jumped into my arms. We looked at each other, then burst out laughing like children.

We went back to the sitting room, me carrying the manuscript under my arm. Without even glancing at it, I began to talk to Ossiana about author's rights and what sort of contract would be best. She interrupted me.

"Edward, I'll do whatever you think is right."

I took the contract that I had brought for *The Need to Love* out of my briefcase and simply changed the language where appropriate, initialing where necessary. Ossiana then signed it, thereby according Turner Press exclusive rights to the complete works of C. Irving Brown, on terms very favorable to her. Then I wrote her out a check for five thousand pounds for the rights to *The Need to Love* — the same amount I had paid to Anthony Ramsay. She was so happy. I could have almost taken her into my arms.

Sitting in the train taking me back to London, I began to read the yellowing pages of Chatterton's manuscript. It reminded me of Nicolas's early works, the kind of things he did when he had not yet become famous. Their voices were similar — the cadence of the sentences, the high-spirited insolence. How moved I felt by the mysterious harmony between the works of these two dead men, whose destinies I had brought together.

Of course, the novel was hardly ready for immediate publication. It required a great deal of work before it approached the level of *The Need to Love*. The work gave me a feeling of freedom, of creative joy, that far surpassed anything I would have ever dreamt possible. Finally, rebirth!

What a glorious morning it is! The boxwood hedges in Hyde Park are giving off a sweet, musky odor. Ossiana has just told me over the telephone that she will spend a few days with me on the Isle of Wight. Her neighbor will see that her greyhounds are cared for. *Only the Journey Matters* is at the printers (the French edition, published by Laurent Millagard, will appear later this autumn), and everyone impatiently awaits this second work by C. Irving Brown. This "resurrection" has transformed my hatred to mercy. I have given this unknown writer posthumous fame to rival that of Leo Perutz, Rupert Brook, and Elizabeth Holden.

I am putting together a small collection of poems. I think I know how to live without Nicolas now. My memory of him dims with each passing day. My demons have fled, and stretching before me are green fields and pastures new.